4024

DATE DUE

The Polish Lover

The

Polish

Lover

～

ANTHONY WELLER

Marlowe
New York

Published by
Marlowe & Company
632 Broadway, Seventh Floor
New York NY 10012

Library of Congress Cataloging-in-Publication Data

Weller, Anthony, 1957-
The Polish lover / by Anthony Weller.
p.   cm.
ISBN 1-56924-738-2 (cloth)
I. Title.
PS3573.E4569P6   1997
813'.54—dc21   97-24367
CIP

ISBN 1-56924-738-2

Manufactured in the United States of America

for

Chris Baumer
&
David Erlanger

and in remembrance of Alex Ullmann
(1958–1992)
who offered his glee

When the moon rises and women in flowery dresses are
    strolling
I am struck by their eyes, eyelashes, and the whole
    arrangement of the world.
It seems to me that from such a strong mutual attraction
The ultimate truth should issue at last.

—Czeslaw Milosz

Soon or late Love is his own avenger.

—Lord Byron

B ecause I am a jazz musician, used to things going wrong, I went to Poland for the holidays.

I am talking about the old Poland, the one you see before you adjust the horizontal hold on the television in your mind: the Poland where people lined up in the cold for two hours just to buy toothpaste or a notepad. I didn't go there to make music, or to learn about politics. I went with a woman. I'll call her only Maja. If I give her full name—who knows?—some European musicians' union might arrest her and assemble a tribunal of horn players.

I should've been able to resist her, or at least question what we were doing. I am a clarinettist: careful by instinct, classical by training, jazzer by first love. Not everyone realizes the clarinet is the subtlest, most portable and agile reed of all—usually it knows how to look out for itself.

For a decade now, trying to explain Maja in memory, I

have told myself that I used her as an excuse to propel my life across the Atlantic. But the other day, for the first time in years, I happened to listen to a recording I made while I was with her, and before I knew it Maja came flowing back at me from my own music like a flesh-and-blood apparition—grinning, arguing, with all her long-legged abracadabra intact. As I listened, our days and nights together emerged in a senseless jumble, and I realized I couldn't reconcile the two Majas I'd known: the woman I fell in love with, and the other Maja I accompanied to Poland.

And after all this time, I'm not sure I can fathom what made me abandon a snug, directed existence in New York—gigs, friends, lessons with a composer, an agent who regularly booked me on tour overseas—for a woman I barely knew. To find myself hunched, shivering in a decrepit Mercedes crawling along a snowbound Polish country road with night falling. In a Christmas fog so impenetrable you couldn't see your hand when you stuck it out of the window, much less the broken tail lamps of the next car or the looming ghost of a farmer's wagon.

It wasn't my Polish beauty beside me, though, trying to steer us through the fog. Instead it was Wojciech, an ex-lover of hers from long before—his lean face framed by lank hair shoved around his ears like Chopin.

"A brilliant poet, you'll see," Maja had assured me that same morning back in Warsaw, as we watched Wojciech haggle in the snow for another can of black market petrol. A few days earlier he had offered us both a ride to Cracow, where he was planning to visit his most serious mistress and their two sons. But soon Maja began suggesting I accompany Wojciech alone on this expedition while she stayed behind at her friend Lena's flat, and I could only wonder where she and I were going wrong.

Meanwhile, I was sure that Wojciech and I could not be lost in the fog, since there was only this one road.

We passed dangerously close to a horse cart at the roadside, the driver and his animal expelling clouds of breath simultaneously. Wojciech shouted something, the fellow yelled back. Wojciech beamed and lit a cigarette, offering me one and then remembering.

"He say we don't get to Cracow. Not tonight." Wojciech waved his hand at the chaos of it all. "Never."

He was about my age, doing graduate studies in philosophy and looking for someone to translate his poems into English. I'd encountered him the week before, soon after Maja and I arrived in Warsaw and people from her past began to drop by, bickering and gossiping over Lena's endless glasses of tea and vodka.

I was still looking for someone who spoke enough English to explain Maja's sudden behavior to me. So far Wojciech and I shared only about a hundred words and a perhaps contradictory knowledge of her, since we knew her in different languages. For hours now the fog had carried us along in silence, like a white glove that had closed around the car.

"You want music? Tapes?" asked Wojciech.

Without waiting for a reply he reached into his jacket pocket and pulled out exactly what I feared most, a homemade cassette that had plagued me ever since the first evening he'd come by Lena's flat. It was a tape of a tape of a tape, worn out through constant use, of the Andrews Sisters—or so Wojciech claimed. It was certainly some women's singing group doing fifties arrangements; I doubted Wojciech understood the syllables he sang along with.

At Lena's he would shove the cassette into her stereo no matter whether the television was on, or people were chatting or listening to some other music. He would turn the volume up and smile beatifically, as if the Andrews' aerated harmonies satisfied some unutterable need in his soul for cotton candy. I couldn't tell if the others good-naturedly put up with Wojciech's whims or genuinely enjoyed this American fluff played over and over.

He turned up the volume in the car as the sisters began their caterwauling. I turned it down slightly. He turned it up again.

"Other car hear us," he said, gesticulating. "Much danger, then they hear us, no danger! Andrews girls on road to Cracow!"

He laughed and tapped in rhythm on the wheel.

I said, "How does Maja seem to you?"

"You know her long time?"

"Ten months."

"She is—" He halted. "Not same, you know. She go all over world, come back to Poland." He joggled his head like someone putting on airs. "Like movie star now. Pretend movie star."

"Maybe in Polish," I said. "Not in English."

He shrugged and peered ahead. In the fog we were managing about ten miles an hour.

"Like cold of clouds, all across car, all across earth," he intoned gravely, peering over hands gone bloodless from gripping the wheel. He darted a look at me and smiled. "Is beautiful sentence, in Polish."

I said, "In English also. It's a fine sentence."

He nodded reverently and glanced at me again, then recited, "German car is old man at last. German car has no more eyes in Polish winter."

He flicked the feeble headlights off and on a couple of times to demonstrate how little difference they made against the fog. I thought: In Polish cold of clouds, American musician is going blind.

I first met Maja at the end of a long tour, near the end of the previous winter, but in New Zealand—"at the other end of the alphabet for both of us," as she put it—her accent like a horse clip-clopping through snow. I was twenty-seven.

The tour had been a costly war of attrition, with surprising rewards. We lost a guitarist, a drummer, and a trombonist in the course of a three-month Pacific campaign. One through illness, one through a better offer, one through an unexpected divorce proceeding back in New York. We began as a sextet in Hong Kong for Halloween, celebrated Thanksgiving in Singapore as a quintet, blew in the New Year at Adelaide as a quartet, and ended up a trio of piano, bass, and clarinet way down in Christchurch, South Island, New Zealand, in late February—their summer.

By tour's end we were practically breathing together, like

some alert foraging animal with three heads. With each musician you lose, your own solos are forced to expand and grow, and by now I was as deep in my playing as Mark and Rob were in theirs, deeper than I'd ever gone. The incandescent nights came regularly now, nights when the instrument is totally on your side, and the ideas are almost all fresh, quickening under your fingertips—nights when you know you're not crazy to have chosen this way of life.

My friends loped off to Bali to have the last month massaged out of their spines. I hung around our Christchurch hotel—the final gig—for a couple of days, catching up on sleep. I wasn't sure what I wanted to do before heading home. No one was expecting me; I had no work back in the States before the middle of March, until an awful Mississippi riverboat shuffle for Japanese tourists that I somehow let myself get roped into every year.

And I remember wanting to explore this new country I'd come to in my playing. Whenever I reach a different plateau with the clarinet, I dream of taking a room in an anonymous place for a month and simply practicing—not only solidifying the progress made, but going back to an initial relationship with music that sometimes gets lost. Playing an instrument often seems a series of skirmishes and retreats and battles for terrain: you try to enjoy the rare stretches of peace as much as possible.

In the end I decided to take a week off in Port Stilton, a little sketch of a town by a glittering lake of the same name, down the coast fifty miles and just inland—I'd seen it pictured on brochures. Perhaps thirty shops and a half-dozen hotels were set in a neighborly way along one edge of the lake, with forested crags looming all around. I took a room at a hotel that resembled an old hunting lodge in the Canadian Rockies where I'd gigged years earlier.

But after two nights there I was more tired than when

I'd arrived. I was sleeping badly; I hadn't reckoned on the natural letdown which follows a long tour. Suddenly your plans for the next day are gone with your colleagues, and you're forced back on your own powers alone, wondering what to do with this shock of empty time every evening that used to be all self-discovery. Abruptly my tour added up to little besides cash and unanswered questions: for example, after months of hard work, playing stronger than ever, was I in fact any closer to getting out a record of my own than a year ago?

I suppose I was feeling a bit lonely, too—a halfhearted regret I hadn't accompanied the other two to Bali. I'd had no steady girlfriend in my life for ages, not since breaking up with a pretty blond journalist named Isabel who worked part-time at a Soho sculpture gallery. She would smile, tell me solemnly that jazz was a parched, dying, irrelevant music, then pester me about coming along on tour. It took months of her complaining about how late I joined her after gigs before I realized how little improvisation—which is pure joy—there was in her.

My second morning in Port Stilton I was walking through the lobby, on my way to the lake, when I noticed a tall woman in shorts, carrying a towel, by the reception desk. She stood with her back to me, looking over the postcard rack. Her straight brown hair was cut boyishly, almost impudently, just above her shoulders; large red-framed sunglasses hid her expression as I passed, but her profile was serene and confident even at a distance. She wore a baggy black sweater (sleeves pushed up to her elbows in the morning heat) that gave no hint of her upper body, and her tanned legs in green shorts made her look even taller, sleeker, simply standing there. She seemed solitary and happy. I guessed she might be thirty.

I walked slowly out, tempted to buy a postcard too, then

stopped for a moment in the sunshine of Port Stilton's only road, wondering if she could be here by herself.

I took my time choosing among the wooden chairs ranged along the narrow beach. It was the usual setup by a lake. Kids were leaping with suicidal whoops off a pier, a man in full tropical kit was fishing, several fleshy middle-aged couples were chattering away in strained hysterical tones or reading in sun chairs. When the woman came out of the hotel and crossed the road, she obviously knew exactly where she was going, and chose a spot as far down the beach from the others as possible.

The lake water was chill this early in the day, so I had a brisk swim past where she was sitting. She hadn't budged, she hadn't taken off any clothes, she hadn't removed her sunglasses. She paged idly through a magazine, not really reading. Then, as I headed back, she took a flat black object out of her shoulder bag, set it on her chair arm, and began staring, her chin on her hand, like someone confronting bad news they can neither believe nor alter.

I swam back as far as my clothes, dried myself vigorously, and realized I'd chosen a place directly in the shade. In search of something sunnier I walked past the few occupied chairs, crossing a frontier into this woman's private province. As I sat down, a couple of empty chairs between us, I realized she was gazing at a foldout chess set. She was concentrating on some endgame problem; only a few magnetic pieces were clustered on the compact board.

I opened my paperback. I didn't look at her, nod a hello, or acknowledge her existence in any way. Still, I shouldn't have been surprised when she spoke.

"Are you following me?" she said.

"I beg your pardon?"

"You're swimming here and then you're walking here."

"Why would I be following you?"

She said, as if she truly couldn't imagine why (and now I realized I couldn't identify that cloaked accent), "Well, that's just what I'm asking myself. Why should this strange man be following me?"

"There's nothing strange. I wanted a sunnier spot. The water's cold today."

"That's not such cold water. But," she added, conceding me something, "this is the best place to sit. I sit here every day."

I told Maja my first name, she told me hers; pronounced like the lost race, it could've come from almost anywhere. She added with old-world politeness, "I'm very pleased to have met you, Danny. You've just arrived?"

"The day before yesterday. And you?"

"Almost three weeks. I'm not allowed to be employed. So I stay on vacation. I have a friend who lives here."

From the way she said *friend* I knew exactly what she meant.

"Is there much to do here?"

"For most people the lake is enough." She gestured with her women's magazine, which was called *Glee*. "But there's no library. And until last week it rains every day. Like—" She paused, wanting to get it right. "Like nonstop dogs and cats."

"And the chess?"

"Do you play?"

"I used to play reasonably well, I guess. I never really studied the game."

"You used to play well but you never studied?" I couldn't tell from her expression how much she was teasing me. "Then we must play a game. After I solve my problem. I don't find anyone here who plays."

She set *Glee* aside and pulled off her sweater, revealing a faded T-shirt that said MONTREUX JAZZ. I saw the shy puckerings of her breasts when she laid her sweater on the chair beside her.

Just my luck, I thought. The lovely jazz fans are invariably spoken for. I said, "I can't place your accent."

"I can hear you're American, no? So you ought to be able to guess my location."

"Vienna, maybe."

"Austria? Next you'll say Germany."

"All right. Not the USSR?"

In those days it still existed.

"Don't insult me," she said with delight. "You really can't guess? My English must be improving. I'm from Poland. Warsaw."

"No kidding," I said. "So am I."

"You're not!"

"Two generations back. My mother's parents. Not Warsaw, though. Cracow."

"You've visited? No? You must go one day. Beautiful city—I have many friends there."

"Maybe the next time I'm in Europe," I said. "When were you at the Montreux festival?"

"Never. I always dream to go, though."

"I nearly played there last summer."

"And this year?"

"Oh, my agent said they lost my tape. Who knows? You can never tell who's not telling you the truth."

"Now you really do sound Polish," she said with a grin, and took off her sunglasses—her eyes were dark brown, with an intense intriguing glitter. "I had plenty of experience with people who don't tell the truth. The only secret I ever discover is you must learn exactly the percentage they tell. And the most dangerous ones are always directly in the middle."

Without the sunglasses her face came alive and softened,

as if she'd been in hiding and quietly decided to give herself
up. There was assurance in her gaze, however, and the
poise of her mouth, which took on a mild surprise when
she smiled.

She said, "I had a Polish boyfriend who played at Montreux twice. He gave me this shirt. Perhaps you know him.
Rzupinski?"

"Alto sax, I think."

"Also the tenor saxophone."

"I heard him on a recording a while back. Strong
player."

"Very strong."

"Is he still in Poland?"

"He must be."

"I'd like to look him up if I ever get there."

"You can try. But he's never easy to locate. He always
finds himself too many problems, that man."

Her tone was full of affectionate regret. It bothered me
a little that she hadn't yet asked me what instrument I
played. We looked across the lake together—the surface
ruffled by the faintest breeze. Then Maja did ask.

A violinist friend of mine, full of classical theory, used to
claim that in a love affair, everything to come is contained,
even expressed, in your first meeting. A woman, he argued,
decides in the first half hour, the first minute perhaps, not
only if she'll sleep with you, but exactly how much more
you might ever mean to her; and as in an orchestral audi-
tion, you must get it right from the beginning. Assuming,
of course, she's not already taken.

Thus with nothing to gain or lose that first morning with
Maja, I found myself rambling on about my Polish grandfather. I'd seen him only once or twice, when I was very
small. My earliest memory was of being plumped on his

lap in front of a piano (a dapper white-haired gentleman in round spectacles and a blue suit) and watching his hands wade up and back along the keys as if through snowdrifts. The story at home, of course, was that my talent had come from him.

He'd left Poland for England just after the First World War—my mother was brought up a Londoner—succeeded there as a lady's tailor, and retired to Israel. But before leaving Poland he'd been a serious musician: originally a pianist, then a composer, trained at the Cracow Conservatory. I enjoyed imagining him in a frustrated middle age, hurrying down the Charing Cross Road in a distinguished overcoat of his own design, muttering to himself in Polish against a chafing London wind, and stopping to jot down a fragment of melody in a small music notebook which my mother remembered he always kept in one particular pocket.

I said, "I have this idea of looking up his old compositions at that conservatory. Do you suppose it's still standing?"

"Cracow was never bombed," said Maja. "Because the Nazis made it their capital. I think the music school must still be there. But probably the Nazis destroyed all the old papers. They didn't tolerate Polish music, you know. Not even Chopin."

"Do you get to Cracow often?"

"Every year. But I haven't decided how long I stay here. I even could be leaving soon, I can't tell."

"Back to Poland."

"Back to Amsterdam. That's my home now, since five years. I've got a small flat. My books. My clothes." She hesitated at the acute recollection of all she'd left in Holland. "Everything. I gave up a good job, in a television studio. Thinking to move here. So I'm afraid I'll not be able to have it back."

"And your friend?"

"Simon? This is his country. He'll stay here. And prob- ably—probably me also. In the end." She paused. "What would you do?"

I wasn't sure how seriously she was asking—I couldn't see myself, or her for that matter, living here for very long, but I didn't want to say so. I said lamely, "I tend to keep moving all the time. I'm on tour a lot."

Meaning I'd spent two months the previous year in a quartet, for instance, playing on an ocean liner making "the dipso-calypso run" around the duty-free rip-off ports of the Caribbean. Practicing Brahms in a closet-sized cabin so near the engines that every sustained tone came out qua- very. Still, it was better than a Manhattan winter, even if the ship went around in circles.

She said with a knowing smile, "But you must have a girlfriend at home, no?"

"Not since June."

She glanced at her little chessboard. She said wryly, "Try again," and budged a magnetic piece with one finger. It was curious to hear American expressions in that accent, like baroque pastries in her mouth. She regarded her end- game solution for a moment, then abruptly snapped the chess set shut. *"Finito!* Now I can swim. Then you and I will play for an open ticket away from here. All right?"

She didn't expect a no. She stood up and stared at me for a moment, like a distant relative trying to decide what she thought of me. Then she squinted across the lake, put her hands to her hips, slid out of her green shorts to expose the sleek black V of a bikini bottom, and in one motion turned away and pulled off her T-shirt and dived cleanly into the lake.

I had a fat paperback with me, a history of the Second World War. For self-improvement. I kept trying to read as

Maja swam past steadily, inexorably. I wonder now which was more persuasive—her challenging voice and eyes and body? Or her mystical passport, the glamour that political suffering bestows on people whose countries we've never visited? Because I knew about Maja's friend, because the tour was over but my real life still a hemisphere away, I could watch her backstroke in half a bikini, let myself dream harmlessly, and feel prickings of family loyalty.

It seemed natural: I was on tour with her and a tough Polish rhythm section in her (our) ramshackle country. In old towns and plaintive villages, in little cafés shrouded by cigarette smoke, the knotted faces of the other Europe were attentive as I played them the news from New York, and I could close my eyes and hear the swaying music clearly. All this came to me in an easy inconsequential improvisation as Maja swam back and forth, back and forth. I kept returning to my paperback.

She waited until chapter two before rising languorously out of the water some distance up the shore, away from everyone, so I had the choice of either watching her approach or else pretending to read about the burning of the Reichstag. Beat to beat, Maja's portamento walk was joyous to behold—like listening to a great cellist play a melody slowly, dreamily, without a break in the sound. I watched her bemused smile as she came closer and wondered sadly if I would ever be a real virtuoso, and why so many American women walk like lumberjacks.

She dried herself only cursorily before sitting down again; her T-shirt glued itself happily to her skin. She said, "Can you borrow me your book when you leave? I've run out. It's all I do in this place, swim and read. I turn into an automaton, but my English at least improves." She raked her wet dark hair back through her fingers. "But you speak English already. What are you doing here?"

I explained I was recovering from a grueling tour, and added a few musician-catastrophe stories—a bad gig acquires prestige if you shift it from a New Jersey nightclub to the Gunpowder Bar at the Hong Kong Hilton. It didn't occur to me that for a Pole who'd never visited the States, Atlantic City could seem as exotic as the Far East.

To improvise is to live: but when you improvise, do you lie, or are you truthful? As a musician my nature was to tell the truth, to try to avoid the facile phrases that lay easily under the fingers, even if it meant missing what I was reaching for. With a woman I doubted I'd ever see again yet wanted to impress, it was too easy to fib, to glibly play the world-touring musician. Ever after (though Maja wasn't fooled) they worried me, those few altered stories at the outset.

"But you should do more concerts, no?" she asked. "Not hotels and clubs. And then you can be appreciated. This is what jazz musicians in Europe do, more than in America, I think. Because European people are habituated to listen to music without drinking and talking. Anyway, you must be very tired after all those hotels." As if pulling back from her sally in my direction, she added soberly, "I heard all about things that go wrong at hotels. Simon's the restaurant manager where you're staying. I'm sure you've seen him. Very tall. With blond hair."

Every mention of that lucky man broke her otherwise direct gaze.

"Have you known him a long time?"

"We lived together in Amsterdam. Two years. Then he lost his permission to work so he came back here in October. We were thinking to break up then. But Polacks are very loyal, you see." She paused. "So I joined him at the end of last month. For another serious try."

Why push a pointless flirtation with her? I didn't have a chance: she was simply being friendly.

She'd been setting the magnetic chess pieces in place as she spoke. She said, "In Warsaw when I was a teenager, I used to gain money playing against American tourists in the old square. If I lost they were always too nice to take money from a Polish girl. But usually I won. So, are you ready?"

"I should probably get in a little clarinet practice before lunch."

"Aha. Well, I understand. If you don't mind it, I'd like to hear you practice one day."

"It's pretty boring. Mostly scales and strange exercises."

"Sometimes the strangeness is more interesting. When Rzupinski and I were together he would practice all day long. Eight, ten hours every day. He said he always practiced better when I was there."

"He might've said that just to make you feel good."

"I decide this also," she said. "But it was nice to believe. Look, you don't have to do an enormous concert for me, you know."

"I'll be glad to really play for you sometime. But you have to promise to let me win once at chess."

"I'm here every morning. No opponents."

I pulled on my shorts and T-shirt. I said, "Do you suppose Rzupinski still practices eight hours a day?"

Maja smiled. "Not the way he used to."

Funny, but all I let myself think as I walked away was: What an unusual person to wash ashore here, I wonder if I'll run into her again.

Lena's flat in Warsaw was an enormous converted attic above the seventh story of an aging apartment building that had survived the war. Maja and I arrived one night a week before Christmas. It hadn't yet snowed, and the city stood gray and gaunt, starved by the inadequate streetlamps.

Lena's building presented a commanding facade on one of Warsaw's broad tram-bisected avenues, but you entered off a side street, past a ceramics shop where the pavement was missing and the way always muddy, via a huge black iron door like the entrance to a tomb. When it slammed shut you found yourself standing in a main entryway of utter darkness and damp. On one stony wall a switch with a stingy timer set off a dim bulb on the first landing of a staircase. You just had time to make out a tiny jail of an elevator, paint peeling like dead skin, a pool of water beneath a dripping pipe, and wiring everywhere—the entire electrical system exposed like intestines.

Yet the building felt permanent, weighty; the staircase was almost grand, with a thick wooden bannister; it'd obviously been an elegant address once. (I imagined formerly well-to-do families at the end of their savings and their ancestral trees.) Eventually I learned to trust the grinding elevator, whose tortured ascents were audible throughout the building. Its single bulb had been stolen and no one wanted to risk replacing it: we rode up to Lena's in darkness.

Lena was long divorced, lived alone, and apparently traveled freely. She was around fifty, but carried herself like a younger woman, as if she were Maja's only slightly elder sister. She must've been beautiful once; her peering green eyes were full of questions and still the occasional flash of flirtation, though she wore her brown hair pulled back rather severely. She seemed addicted to clove cigarettes. She dressed with a deliberate air of independence: blue jeans, boots, a silk blouse and baggy wool sweater, a leather coat. Maja told me that years ago they'd been rivals for a boyfriend—I assumed the more experienced woman had won.

Lena refused to practice her bad English on me, so we spoke French, in which I stumbled along like a schoolboy. She'd contrived somehow (I never got much explanation for how certain Poles managed these coups) to own a cottage in the French Midi and spent several months there every year; in fact a couple of neighbors with two children would be coming by train from Paris for the holidays.

Her attic flat took a whole floor and received the reluctant light of many small windows. According to Maja, the huge eyrie was by Warsaw standards almost unthinkable, and full of treasures you simply couldn't get in Poland. Turkish rugs and Moroccan pillows, Indian fabrics, and

South American blankets lay scattered all about. Lena had covered the slant ceilings with narrow wood panels; a massive brick fireplace and elaborate Chinese screens divided the flat into territories. One dominated by a long wooden dining table that you might've imagined at a French country house, another by a tilted drafting table with clothing designs and a modern study lamp. There were deep sofas and armchairs between the windows, and a well-equipped kitchen area near the door, though the stove was ancient. A distinguished desk in one corner held higgledy-piggledy files and a black telephone. It rang often and Lena always looked worried when she crossed the flat to reach it—I think she had an estranged daughter somewhere on the loose in Europe.

Beyond the chimney was a screened-off canton where Lena slept, and the sole bathroom. A back passage had a little sleeping loft and led to a final room where Maja and I shared an uncomfortable floor mattress by a paint-stained sink and another drafting table. Dozens of science fiction canvases by a painter friend of Lena's leaned in a clutter against the exposed brick walls; apparently she sometimes represented him abroad. I never learned what Lena actually did for a living, if she did anything.

According to Maja, Lena got over to New York whenever she wanted and sold her one-of-a-kind clothing to a few select shops there. They were always clamoring for more, Maja said, but Lena designed only when it suited her.

I offered to pay for Lena to design a dress for Maja for Christmas. This amused them both.

"What should the dress look like?" said Maja. "You have an idea?"

It was our second day in Poland. Exactly one week before, after six years in New York, I'd turned over the keys to my apartment and hopped a plane to Amsterdam with three suitcases, a trunk of music, my two best clarinets, and seven thousand dollars my landlord had given me in return for moving out. I was still stunned by what I'd done, stunned by a sterile few days in windy Amsterdam at the flat Maja borrowed from a Dutch doctor whose Polish wife had left him ages ago.

Before that week I'd never seen Maja in winter clothes— her long body concealed in corduroys and a thick sweater as brown as her hair. They made her one with the bundled-up people I'd watched skitter along during our walk yesterday, these people who had no money yet all had odd luxuries, like fur coats and little mink hats and leather bags. Until a freezing rain began we'd braved the wind along a tree-lined avenue with ornate, belle epoque embassies on both sides, then caught an unheated tram back to the flat.

"*Plzlkmdzry*," said Lena to Maja, who laughed in that full-bodied way I loved—like someone finding an unexpected bottle of good wine in the cupboard. I didn't ask for a translation; I'd already decided to stay out of the way while Maja enjoyed her first visit home in nearly two years. This was my Christmas present to her, since Maja hadn't found steady work again back in Amsterdam.

"Lena thinks," said Maja, "that you must be careful. So just because you like the designs she did for me ten years ago, perhaps you don't like the style of what she would do for me now. And they are *very* expensive."

I understood this last was to impress me and see if the American would inquire *how expensive*. It's a cheerful game Poles like to play with us.

"I'd still like to see some of her recent designs," I said.

"You shouldn't be so sure," said Lena to me in French. "People change." She added something else I didn't catch. At my puzzlement she ran off a stream of Polish and Maja nodded, then got up to put a kettle on the stove, her voice trailing as she sauntered away.

"Lena said—" Her words disappeared behind the chimney. "She said people's ideas about beauty change. They fall in love with an idea for a little while and then go somewhere else. So you must be careful always when you ask someone like a painter to do something beautiful for you. Not to expect what you have loved from them before."

I said to Lena, "I'm a musician, you know. I understand this." But I sounded like someone protesting, not agreeing.

"I think you'd better have some strong Polish tea," Maja called out. "For us, truth is in tea, not wine."

There were always visitors at Lena's flat. Occasionally they telephoned; usually they simply appeared, like the small knotted man with a bony face who wouldn't take off his overcoat.

Lena didn't introduce him by name, but as an electronics repairman. Did I want to change some dollars?

At the airport I'd changed a hundred bucks, the minimum, at an official government rate of about 160 *zlotys*. Before I could answer Lena, the electronics man pulled wads of Polish money from several interior coat pockets and began counting out a colossal stack. He could offer me about 950 *zlotys* to the dollar—the black market was running at six times the government rate.

The transaction was accomplished swiftly, the man nodded a thank-you and left. I felt mingled guilt and satisfaction. Guilt, I suppose, that I was by far the stronger party in that situation; satisfaction that I'd come out so well, my jeans pockets stuffed with *zlotys*. I'd an idea to buy myself some handmade leather boots.

"You look so unhappy," said Maja. "You shouldn't feel bad. He is pleased to have met you. It's safe because you're with Lena. He would get into heavy trouble if he got caught doing this with a tourist. Now he can get batteries and parts he needs from Germany."

"My dollars cost him a lot of money."

"His customers will pay," she said.

Lena said, "He's been waiting for you two for a week now. And he got a better rate from you than a money-changer would give."

Yet I wondered if the two women weren't both, in their different ways, outside the Polish loop: this man's problems, surely, weren't theirs.

I offered Maja some of my wad of *zlotys*.

"I'll see my father later on," she said. "He will give me plenty. He always does. He saves it up all year until I come. It satisfies him to pay for me when I'm here." She shrugged. "Here he is a successful man, so he can help me. What he gives me for a week in Warsaw doesn't buy two dinners in Amsterdam, so when I leave I hand him back the rest of my *zlotys*. But I don't think he gets it."

"He knows the rates, surely. He knows it's a different scale in the West, no?"

"He understands the mathematics," she said. "Still, it's all abstract to him. He hasn't left Poland since he was a young man. Before the war. He doesn't see that behind the abstract, there's something else that's real. So he gives me *zlotys* here, and it makes him happy. And I make it clear I don't need any help outside of his country."

"But it's your country too, no? And you need all the help you can get."

"We all do," she said. "But it's not my bloody country. Not anymore."

_____ (PORT STILTON)

One reward of playing an instrument is
that after years of practice, many tech-
nical exercises become routine, even automatic. If you actually had to concentrate scrupulously on every note while
running, say, a pattern in chromatic thirds across twelve
keys for maybe the nine thousandth time in your life, it
would drive you mad.

So, arpeggiating in my New Zealand hotel, giving my
attention to the view—over a blue-and-white striped awn-
ing to the lake, people lying like languid corpses on the
sand—I found myself considering this woman I'd met the
day before. That morning there'd been a note downstairs
suggesting I join her and her friend for dinner that evening.
She hadn't appeared at the beach, though.

I thought also about how I never stayed in one place for
very long. I still tolerated New York, even after five years,
but only because I left regularly. I loved having the freedom

to go anywhere with a small, weighty instrument case, pop open the clasps, fit the reed, and make a living. I enjoyed constant motion, making up music as I went along, with an individual sound I'd bought from my body. It satisfied me to come back to jostling Manhattan after a week or a month away, to have my friends tell me I'd missed nothing.

And yet after this tour, after three months on the other side of the world, I had to ask myself if New York was really the best base of operations. It's difficult, however, to persuade a serious jazzer that he should operate from anywhere else. What were my other choices? Los Angeles for the studios, Nashville for the country scene—assuming bluegrass clarinet ever caught on—where else? Boston, where my parents live, doesn't count much anymore, unless you want to teach or compose; Miami doesn't count anymore, unless you want to tan.

I wondered, though, if I was kidding myself about having a center. I saw a shadowy succession of selves scattered like birds across the world, aimlessly fluttering into darkness. I had no big career in progress—most record company types think the clarinet belongs in a coffin—and with few exceptions, a good career in jazz means years of come-and-go gigs, then you die. I knew I was establishing nothing behind me anywhere, making no mark. Music came out of silence and went back to silence: sometimes what struck me most about it was the vanishing.

And being away so long reinforced the fact that I didn't have anyone to return to. My Manhattan apartment was proportioned for one person who got along well with himself. It was just off Third Avenue in what remained of York-ville, on the obscure wastes of the Upper East Side—four blocks from the museums, hair salons, and elegant butcher shops of the rich. I was living on a frontier among penny-pinching Korean grocers, young investment bankers with patrician haircuts, and elderly German, Hungarian, Yugo-slavian, and Ukrainian emigrés waiting out their final years in frustration, battening sourly on rent control.

These were the only ones I felt any alliance with—every musician is a kind of refugee. It would scrape at my heart to see those aged immigrant ladies with filmy eyes, shuffling around the corner in bedroom slippers and overcoats to buy their old-world blinis or sauerkraut or sip goulash among their fellow jetsam of the war, as if they still possessed our neighborhood. An elderly couple who'd learned little English lived directly above me; I used to hear them quarreling down the air shaft in a garbled language I couldn't identify, but alone of all my neighbors they didn't seem to mind my practicing. Not that my neighbors' complaints ever stopped me. In New York you learn that a certain amount of ill will, which they call grief, gets you through the day.

Much of the immigrant population of my part of the city had already been forced out by wave after wave of career-ing young men and women, carrying attaché cases and destroying neighborhoods with their hygienic bars, their lifeless Chinese restaurants, their humming (B flat) high-rise apartment blocks like gigantic air-conditioning units. They had equal ignorance of Coltrane and Chausson, of Pale-strina and Bechet, but a seemingly total recall of sports sta-tistics. I resented the way they had unintentionally, in only a few years, uprooted a whole way of life from the city.

Still, it could be a kind of death to get stuck anywhere, and not just a place as small as this New Zealand settle-ment. I couldn't imagine how Maja, who had come very far to reach this lake, might sustain herself here—but then I hadn't met her friend yet.

She was waiting for me that evening in the hotel lobby, tan in a short shimmering green dress, and alone.

"Simon has to work for two hours more," she said. "You

don't mind just me and you for dinner? Ah, here he is. He insisted to meet you."

He came striding across the lobby, taller than Maja or I, bony in a casual jacket, striking and self-possessed from a distance, rather pensive up close. I put him at about thirty-five. We shook hands and introduced ourselves while Maja said nothing but seemed to watch from the wings with great curiosity. Simon had an occasional stutter; funny how a speech defect makes a person sound sincere. Maja seemed different around him. Subdued, almost held in check.

"Mutiny in the kitchen," he said. "We've got a group in from Hong Kong who weren't due till tomorrow. A b-bloody rebellion over twenty extra plates. You'll be around another day or two, right?"

"At least."

"We should've arranged a concert. None of your group is still with you, eh? Too b-bad, the place could use a good rave-up. Hope you're feeling energetic. This lady's been a dancing fool ever since the dim-and-distant. She warned me she might even treat."

"I'm not much of a dancer," I said.

"You'll find your way, eh? Don't fret, she's explained the situation—I'll see what I can arrange." He winked at me. "I'll catch up with you two at the Happy Gardens. Ever notice how the Chinese make their restaurants sound like a celestial paradise?"

He squeezed her arm and gave me a man-to-man wave, then strode off back to work. Maja and I walked out of the hotel into the fresh night, the lake excited and aglow.

"What situation did he mean?" I asked.

I heard myself sounding rather testy.

"I told him you want to meet some Maori girls and you don't have much time," Maja said conspiratorially. "He can bring someone for you to dance with. All the hotel waitresses trust him, you know. They're special people, the Maoris."

She meant the New Zealanders of Polynesian blood—perhaps she was worried I'd be after her?

She noticed my silence. "Don't tell me that you're not interested. You'll like this restaurant. Chinese, but everyone dances there tonight until late."

I said, "Of course I'm interested. I'm famished."

"Famished? This means cold or hungry,. something like that."

"Weren't we talking about dinner?"

"I understand you very well. You'll see, the Maoris are the only interesting people here. The white Kiwis call them lazy islanders. But the Maoris are like a country inside this country. They've got nothing left, no religion, no land. Only ancestors and their language. Poland was that way once, all cut up in other countries. We had religion instead of ancestors. But we became a country again. And the Maoris don't mind waiting, either. You don't think the Maori girls are beautiful?"

"Some of them are."

The lake rustled like aluminum foil, tarnished by moonlight.

I said, "Look, you're going to let me treat you to dinner. No matter what Simon says."

"No," she said firmly. "I will pay for my own. So you don't get the wrong idea."

"What would that be?"

She said with sudden sharpness, "He jokes that I can't pay for a meal. All because he bought my plane ticket here and he pays maybe for my ticket back. So he insults me with a stranger. It's not my fault they're afraid to give a work permit to a Polack. So I'll pay for both of us, it's better that way."

Not the wrong idea I'd arrived at already.

I said, "Why don't we wait and see who wins at chess? You never know, you might need every penny."

"Oh, I'm not worried about your chess." Her mood could lift in an instant. "I am worried you don't like to dance."

"Of course I'll dance."

"You say that like never. I used to dance for a living, you know. When I first came to A'dam from Warsaw." She gave me a sidelong glance as we walked past the buzzing hotels and a sheepskin shop or two facing the lake. "Maybe we had no fresh fruit sometimes in Poland, but we had good ballet training, at least."

I said, "Were they all as tall as you?"

"Not in Poland. In Amsterdam, yes. But not as desperate. I had no money at all. Twenty guilders. None of the Polacks I knew had any money to help me. I used to move from one old sofa to another. Or the floor. Even a closet, once—I slept on two overcoats for a week. Finally I got a job as a dancer. In a *corps de ballet*."

"I thought you worked in a television studio."

"That was after," she said. "Dancing wasn't bad. I was with a painter friend from Warsaw. Named Saskia. We were laughing all the time. The money was good, too. But you can't dance forever."

Her ambition then, I supposed, had been bureaucratic survival in a new country, the right papers and correct signatures and proper stamps in her passport. What, I wondered, were her ambitions now? Was it a better alternative to Europe, this remote lake with a lozenge of moon fizzing away in it?

The Happy Gardens was probably the Chinese restaurant closest to Antarctica, and certainly the only one in Port Stilton. Candles, sawdust floor, a few meager Chinese New

Year decorations dangling. After we ordered, Maja said, "Now Saskia has got hold of an American guy. He keeps flying to Amsterdam for a week and brings her gifts, then goes back. He's convinced she's a genius painter."

"Is she?"

"With Saskia you never know. She paints constantly. Pictures big like that wall. Sometimes bigger. Very colorful. Lots of paint everywhere."

"So she isn't dancing?"

"Not like before." Maja considered. "She's at a peep show now."

"A peep show?"

"You know—dancing naked in your own aquarium."

Against the little crèche-town and the polished beauty of the lake, the massed shoulders of cliffs with surrounding woods, a world of peep shows and lonely men looking in seemed not squalid but only a folk legend told about the barbarous people of a far country.

I said, "I suppose it pays so she can keep painting. She doesn't ever have trouble with men?"

"She says there's a huge Javanese guy to destroy anyone who tries to bother the girls. Of course Saskia is always in a fight with the heavy Javanese." Maja seemed relieved that I wasn't disapproving of her friend. "The guy keeps some of her tips, so one day she hits him over the head with a radio. Maybe she wanted him to sleep with her and he wouldn't, so she can't forgive him."

Talk to a stranger in the States and you'll find that most of his or her friends seem to be sober-minded people in some ordinary business, both feet on the ground and their eyes on the road. While with anyone from Eastern Europe, after five minutes of conversation you've wandered into a tangle of out-of-work journalists, avant-garde musicians, misunderstood smugglers, untranslated poets, and nude dancers who come after you with heavy objects. They all know or have heard of each other and overflow with stories about ones they haven't ever met. They cannot resist a tightrope and cannot take anything seriously that smells of an established order; after a while you begin to think there is a kind of loyalty in the way they say terrible things about their friends.

Still, they judge a person on the basis of his intentions. It never seems to matter very much to them if the poet hasn't written a line in years or the painter wasn't terribly good or the musician got sacked for not showing up or the journalist has wrecked himself on vodka. Since nearly everyone is a failure in their society, one way or another, there are no "losers" as there are in the States. *Loser* is the ultimate American expression—I always feel that jazz sticks up for losers, tells them not to give in or apologize.

Of course, I hadn't known many Eastern Europeans at that point—a Czech bassist I'd played with once; that genius pianist Makowicz who came over twenty years ago and frightened everyone; and a Hungarian drummer we called Mad Tibor, who was forever erecting ramparts of percussion equipment as if to defend himself against the end of the world. They were visited on gigs by faithful, friendly hangers-on who never spoke much English and seemed impervious to alcohol, and who always turned out to be watchmakers or painting restorers or chess champions. These characters could convert a midtown after-theater supper club into a cellar in Eastern Europe with one round of drinks. I liked their natural distrust of people in established positions, and their instinct for making their own way: they seemed stronger for having no other choice.

I had told Maja how elegant I thought she looked. She said, "A close friend in Warsaw designed this dress for me years ago. It's a very happy memory of our friendship, because afterwards we stopped speaking for a long time."

I didn't feel I should ask why, so I asked about her parents (long divorced, Warsaw; mother a chief secretary in an office, father a sort of vice-president in a factory). There was an older sister, in the army as a career and, I gathered, estranged from the family as a result. Maja had learned English early in school and was well-read in my language. When I asked if she'd been required to learn Russian, she said, "Of course." She had at her fingertips much of her region's poetry and quoted me a passage of Milosz (the living one) in Polish—a ravishing sound, like snow crunching underfoot. Then she translated for me.

> . . . *That girl, does she already suspect*
> *That beauty is always elsewhere and always delusive?*

"Beautiful, no? Would you believe, when I first heard the poem—I was just a little girl, his work was forbidden then—I was sure he meant I could only look beautiful if I was somewhere else."

I said, "Well, you must've been glad to get to the West and be able to dress the way you like." I had visions from newscasts of dumpy Polish women in similar frumpy overcoats on brooding, wind-torn streets.

She said, "That's the surprise. You should see how elegant the women in Warsaw dress. At least they used to. They would drive you mad—you would have been blind from the miniskirts in the summer. And real elegance, not something you buy without imagination from shops. We did the designs ourselves, or copied out of French and Italian magazines. We made the clothes too, or sometimes they came from my mother's tailor. And we didn't have money, either—my mother would pay with supplies she stole from her office. That's how everything gets paid for in Poland. Someone steals from someone else and swaps it for something that's gone missing."

"Do you miss your country?"

"I miss friends. But a lot of them got out. I go back once a year, that's enough. There's no hope for anything there right now. Americans are people with their hopes, French have their hopes, even the Dutches think something will turn out better if they count their change. The Polacks know nothing will happen so they want everything. They believe the world owes them a big debt, every one of them. Even if they know other people are more deprived. You can't live in that mentality. I can't, anyway. No matter what other problems I create for myself somewhere else."

Our dinners came: the worst Chinese food I'd had in months.

"How's the food in Poland?"

She said with a sigh, "Better, perhaps, you never find out."

"Tell me about these other problems," I said.

"If I tell you they won't seem like problems to you."

"I'm sure they would."

"You will say, Ah, but here's what you should do. And you could tell me even the proper solution but it will be in a handwriting I can't read. You see?"

"I'm not sure what you mean."

"I must find it myself. Like the solution to a chess problem. It comes to you on its own, or it doesn't. It's contrary with the rules to look in the back of the book until you try yourself. So I keep quiet until I finish trying. And," she finished cryptically, "I don't look in anyone else's book."

"And then?"

"Then perhaps I write you what my problems were."

"Perhaps it'll be too late. You should tell me now."

"Don't look so gloom," she said. "You remind me of that young man in the novel by Lermontov. About the hero. Gloom? Is that right?"

"Gloomy. Or glum."

I have never read Lermontov.

"Save your glum. Practice your chess. We can dance in a few minutes." She leaned forward. "So tell me about American women. In the Dutch magazines it says they're overweight and neurotic and wear athletic shoes all the time. This can't be true?"

"Why don't you see for yourself?" I said. "If you end up flying back to Europe in my direction, you should stop in New York."

I must've been about as transparent as the wine. She sipped thoughtfully and said, "On the way here I changed planes in Los Angeles. But only for a few hours."

"You could change planes for a few days in New York instead."

"I never tried. And I would need a visa."

"So why not get a visa?"

It's so easy to have this kind of conversation on the other side of the planet.

She regarded me with amusement. "Snap your fingers and pick up the visa? Like Chinese food? I don't have my Dutch passport yet, you see. Not for another two years. And with a Polish passport they ask for the encyclopedia. They want to know if you have a job you're going back to, how much money you have with you, let us see the lease on your flat, let us see your husband. So we know you aren't trying to move to America and disappear." She blinked at me, a kind of bantering double wink I later realized was peculiar to Polish women. "You can't blame them," she added. "They know what it means to have too many Po-lacks."

"You should be a politician."

"I wish all I had to do was come to America to solve my problems. Then I would try seriously."

"I'll write you a letter of invitation. Will that help?"

"After tonight you'll be writing letters for all the Maori girls. Be careful, they're stronger than they look."

"And you?"

She said lightly, almost wistfully, "Older, maybe. Poorer. That means stronger, I think."

The Happy Gardens had gradually filled with people gossiping and drinking, waiting for the music to start. Many were Maoris, beefy men and tall women ripe with South Seas beauty. I was too ensnared by Poland to be distracted by anyplace else.

She said, "We should not wait for Simon if we want to dance. He might be too late."

I hoped he wouldn't appear at all—maybe his kitchen mutiny would engulf the hotel. "There's no music yet," I said.

Just then the lights dimmed melodramatically and music revved up—that sound system could've filled a football stadium. Closing my ears to the noise, I took her hand and she let me lead her to the edge of the dance floor. Then it was she pulling me right through the press of dancers, her hand insistent and intimate, to where we couldn't easily be seen in semi-darkness behind the hurly-burly of jittering bodies.

Her shimmering dress had seemed a bit shapeless when she was sitting down or walking. When she began to dance, in the Chinese candlelight, it was devastating. Its thin straps kept slipping off her shoulders (queen takes pawn, check; mate in two), so to hold it up she was compelled to cinch her arms in, deepening her breasts. As she shimmied, the dress clung and caressed her and sidled high up her thighs.

When the dance finished and she stopped wriggling I snapped out of hypnosis. There was a momentary break in the din and we resumed our seats. She said softly, "It's you who are a dancing fool, no?" Then she drew guiltily away. "Look what Simon's brought for you."

He had a couple of exuberant Maori waitresses from the hotel in tow. Temani, in tight American jeans, offered to get us all beer. Her hefty friend had a name like Mapi or Napi. She gave me a chummy punch on the shoulder; I caught a knowing look from Simon. As the bulldozer music started again Napi grabbed my arm and nearly threw me onto the dance floor. She was graceful but very rowdy, and when our dance ended I was glad that Napi excused herself to toss around someone her own size.

A musician gets accustomed to watching other people dance and how unconsciously they reveal themselves. On the floor, Simon and Maja certainly seemed a couple, but it might've been the dancing of two close friends, not lovers. He could match her energy, but he didn't have her body's wit; it was odd to see her with someone so earthbound. Still, they'd come all this way together. Perhaps she saw a kind of challenge in his solidity—for all I knew the man gave her orders and she willingly obeyed. But when Maja looked away from him, even dancing, he'd glance quickly to where her attention was directed, and I felt a play of possessive force between them.

Probably they were meant for each other. I was wasting my time here, endangering my ears, and the sensible move was to pay our table's bill and go.

I was counting my change when the music ended abruptly. In the gaping silence—intended to sell drinks— Simon and Maja came back, a little out of breath, and sat down.

"You're not leaving, are you?" she said.

"There'll be more activity in the next hour or so," said Simon. "Better stay. You haven't danced with Temani yet."

"She seems to have a friend. And Napi was plenty."

"You haven't danced with me yet," said Maja.

"But the music's run out." I really was ready to leave.

"It'll be back to haunt you in a moment, mate," said Simon. "Maja said you've been traipsing all over Australia and a b-bit of Southeast Asia. My old territory. Pre-Europe, that is. I was over in Penang for a while and then the Barrier Reef for a couple of years. I guess you get around in your line of work, too."

"Not as much as I'd like."

"Keep moving or you die," he said. "That's my credo. Forward motion theory of evolution. We're just lately transported here from the Netherlands. Can't tell how long we'll sit still when it comes to the end of the day. Neither one of us relishes being tied down."

"That explains her dancing."

He said, "It really is too bad you don't have your group with you. Over in Georgetown I could've dug up a good Malay rhythm section for you. We could use a dose of live music around here. Wake some people up." He smiled ruefully. "That's what I miss most from Amsterdam. You could hear music of any sort. Always a b-bargain, too. I suppose it's, on your side, that you musicians aren't paid enough. Not a great living."

"No, but a great life."

He was expressing genuine regret that he wasn't able to hire my trio; I was genuinely annoyed that he thought me unquestionably for hire.

The sound came blasting up again from the floorboards—sheer repetitive noise, with little music in it, still has a momentous effect on people. I seized the quick opportunity to wish them both good night and squeeze through the throng. Noise and light dwindled behind me as the door shut. It was an enormous relief to be out in the crisp air, to see stars placed exactly atop tall pines, to find the moon there where I'd left it in the lake, and to hear that sonic assault, that aural terrorism, reduced to the strangulated murmur of a radio shut in a closet. It surged for an instant as the door opened then was put in its place again.

Walking, I told myself I had no business getting caught up in a hasty desire for a woman who, no matter how interested she seemed, was almost certainly unattainable—who would probably marry this man in a few months, for why else would she stay here? In a few days I'd be back in New York; the dream of a quick adventure with Maja was only my way of pretending the tour wasn't over. I was playing tricks with myself. I had no right starting this petty game, trying to succeed where I could only either fail or do harm.

I walked on slowly, inhaling the night's perfume. There seemed more humanity in this quiet lake than in that human roar—I could almost feel the lake thinking, I could see stray thoughts pass across its surface without being committed to memory.

Purposeful footsteps in the road, then Maja was suddenly beside me, between me and the water.

She kept her voice low. "Why are you leaving so early?"

"I told you. I heard enough noise."

The roar echoed faintly along the road, muffled by the lake.

She said, "Are you going to run away from chess also?"

I surprised myself—and answered Maja—by pulling her toward the shadows. She came along off-balance; with my arm around her waist she reluctantly let me kiss her but did not kiss back.

She regarded me quizzically. "Do you think it's a good idea to stand in the road?"

"No one can see us here."

"They might. Are you going to let me go?"

I drew us back further into the shadows, my arm still around her. She said dubiously, "I really didn't expect you to do this."

"I thought it must be why you followed me."

"There's something I wanted to ask." She loosened my hand and stood back. "How old are you?"

Some chance whim made me lie by a year.

"Twenty-eight. For another few months."

"So you were born in—"

I subtracted a year.

Her eyes gleamed in the moonlight as if I'd struck a match. She put both hands solemnly on my shoulders and, like a secret was about to be wrung from her, held me away at arm's length. She murmured—in that accent, remember, and gazing calmly into my eyes—

"I cannot resist you."

There actually is a God in heaven, I thought, and He looks after His musicians.

"You're just saying that. Prove it."

This time when I pulled us together she gave in, and her body stirred against mine, or was it me stirring? Abruptly she broke the kiss, pushed me away and stepped back into the road.

"Let's keep walking," she said. "Aren't you curious about what I said? I can promise it's not because I think you're clever or good-looking or something like that."

"I didn't think it could be."

She said, "I'll be thirty-three in August. Born in 1952. Do you know what that year signifies in the Chinese system? It means I'm a dragon."

Ah, then I'll be Saint George, I thought. "So what does that make me?"

"You don't know?" She stopped walking. "No one ever told you?"

"I think I saw it once on a menu in Singapore. The Abominable Snowman or something. Right? Or a slug. A Manchurian earthworm."

She said, "Do you always make fun of the reasons you do things? Actually, it makes sense. You're a monkey."

"I might've guessed. I suppose it's too late to change."

"Are you crazy? The monkey is the most intelligent creature of all. It's the only one the dragon can't overcome. Because of the monkey's wisdom and trickery. The monkey knows exactly how to get around the dragon's fire and strength. And in the end the dragon can't resist the monkey."

I was overpowered by the statistical idea of those many millions of men walking the earth, each born a year before me, each fortunate but unknowing, irresistible to Maja.

I said, "Can the monkey resist the dragon, though? I'll bet he can."

She said, "He can surely try. That's not the point. You see, only the monkey is wise enough to help when the dragon's fire fails."

Later I learned, naturally, that I'd been born in the year of the rooster—the stupidest creature of all, strutting around, making a fuss, not realizing he has only a limited role to play.

"What if they're not helping each other? If they're opposed?"

Maja said, "It depends on how fiery the dragon chooses to be. How dangerous."

Moonlight had crawled across the road, and she was careful to stand in it now.

"Are we going swimming tomorrow?" I asked. "Or won't it be safe?"

"I don't think it's too dangerous yet. But perhaps it rains. Anyway, it's for me it would not be safe."

She turned and began to walk back, following the moonlight. Her form shimmered at me.

"Don't get lost," I called out. "There might be monkeys in the trees."

Her laughter rang lightly along the road, but she didn't turn.

_____ (W A R S A W)

Warsaw was a city of dark stone, yet wood was everywhere: scaffolding around buildings under perpetual repair (I never saw any workers) and plank fences encasing empty lots. But pasted to the fences were the most imaginative cinema posters I'd ever seen. Always original, their designs owed nothing to a film's publicity in the West. And there were posters for the dozens of theaters doing Ibsen and Molière and Shakespeare and Chekhov and Pinter and Dostoevsky and Conrad—Poles were ready to adapt anything. Tickets, Maja assured me, were always unavailable.

I remarked how much I loved the posters, how much I saw in them. She said, "I told you, no? An old friend of mine is one of the important painters of them. He has the largest collection of posters, after the government. His own originals, but most from all the other painters. Do you want to meet him?"

She'd mentioned Andrzej months ago—the great love of her life when she was eighteen. He'd been older, with a great future, and stayed behind when his mother fell ill instead of leaving when he had the opportunity. Years later his mother was still alive and he was wasting himself in Warsaw, teaching art, reviewing films, and (she said) turning out fewer and less imaginative posters—one more talent whose life was muddled beyond repair.

"Why doesn't he leave?" I asked. "He must be only forty."

"At forty your life is settled in Poland," said Maja. "We all told him to leave when he was twenty-eight. He didn't have the courage then. He could have done anything, that man. But I am curious to see him—not since two years. We had a big fight the last time. Maybe he still doesn't want to see me."

We went to his flat one afternoon in a taxi. This meant waiting twenty minutes in the cold at a corner taxi stand then sharing a ride with three other people. The driver tried to convince us to pay in dollars, due to my presence.

"What did you fight about?"

In that East German–built taxi you could feel every bump, every gradation of snow matted on the streets.

"He asked me to marry him. After we don't see each other for years. So I said: You're doing everything at the wrong time, my Andrzej. If you want to come to Amsterdam and you need a place to stay, that's all right for a little while. Or even I'll arrange something longer with friends there and I pay. Because I remember the difficulties I had. Instead he wanted me to move in with him back here, in Warsaw. Can you imagine? Then six months later I heard he was married."

Andrzej and his wife lived in a part of town I hadn't

visited yet, with more early-century character than the rest, fewer cars, and almost no Soviet-style buildings. To be away from their oppression was a relief. The sidewalks were wide, the trees stood boldly as in an etching, the snow relieved the unshaven look on the grimy faces of the buildings. As we walked (Maja had mistaken the address), red trams occasionally passed with dim headlights, each like a little train in an old-fashioned children's cartoon, chugging self-importantly along. Here were numerous *antikwariaty*, secondhand bookshops with their meticulous windows of arcane treasures and their proprietors visible inside, sipping tea and stacking frayed Soviet magazines with patriotic peasant beauties on the dusty covers.

Maja said in wonderment, "Do you believe I nearly forgot where he is? And all the months and months I stayed here."

Could he have been as important to her as all that? I thought. She'd always made him sound like a difficult man to misplace.

Eventually she found the narrow building, hidden between two grand demimondaines. In the hallway Maja fumbled for the timer light; it ticked ominously as we went up a narrow staircase that smelled of rainwater, garbage, and urine. "Third floor," said Maja confidently as the light clicked off. She knocked on a door and had to apologize to an ancient war veteran disturbed from a nap.

"Perhaps I really don't want to find him," she murmured.

We heard bustling voices and caught the scent of tea on the next landing. A door creaked, spilling nervous light, and a little man with a beard and ponytail darted out and softly intoned her name. He managed to hug her and wink at me and shake my hand and introduce me to his silhouetted wife, all at the same time.

"Come in, come in," said his wife. "You speak English, yes? I am teacher."

Her name escapes me now, but she seemed a mildly dumpy counterpart of Andrzej himself—an aging jazz fan in jeans and a workshirt with a black turtleneck beneath. He made grand gestures, kept a set of bongos, and had books piled everywhere. A curtain hid one wall in the stifling flat and I knew that behind it would be more books. A dilapidated drafting table was jammed into a corner, its face averted. The ungainly Soviet television looked like a behemoth from the fifties but was "the latest Kremlin model," Maja assured me. As a precaution for when the heat went off, foam rubber was shoved around the windows and a couple were covered by blankets. I was sweating almost immediately.

I saw no theater posters. A dog that resembled a dirty floormop nuzzled my hand then leaped excitedly at Maja. She and Andrzej, standing, seemed to be speaking a little uncomfortably—whenever a Polish conversation was at 16 rpm I assumed something was amiss. His wife meanwhile led me to the best seat in the house, a ragged blue sofa with plump cushions. She sat beside me and said, "You must correct my English if I make mistakes, it's been such a long time since I was in London."

"The hell with that," said Andrzej. He coerced Maja into a chair and said to me, "What do you want to drink? She says you're a jazz musician. Dammit, you can hear whatever you want in this household. Brubeck? Miles? I've got some Louis Armstrong live in Russia that you can't get anywhere. Or maybe you only want vodka and silence, eh? My wife makes too many grammatical errors, you hit her, she won't listen to me. A bitch is a female dog, right? Doesn't want to admit my English is better than hers."

I said, "How about some vodka and Louis?"

"Satchmo martini!"

"I'll get it, just sit," said his wife.

Maja joined her in the narrow kitchenette and left me to fend for myself with Andrzej, who pulled me by the arm to his record collection. Sprawled on two shelves, it looked as if it'd been dragged by a tractor through a field. He insisted I kneel alongside him and, like two praying acolytes, we went through the titles, half of which were in the Cyrillic alphabet—Russian pressings, much of it classical music.

I said, "Are there still stores here where I can get these?"

"Don't be funny," he said under his breath. "There's one store and you can buy everything for the price of ten cheeseburgers in Times Square. What am I looking for?"

"Armstrong in Moscow?"

"Was it Moscow? I thought it was St. Petersburg—they call it something else now. Bolshevik bastards, they don't know what real communism is. I'm only kidding. Forget Louis, I'll find him later. Ever hear this guy?"

He pulled out a record jacket with an inscription scrawled all over it. A fellow about my age, good-looking in a Chet Baker youthful-promise way, holding a tenor saxophone from which flew tiny nude women shaped like eighth notes, their arms flung back. Blurred in the background was a young brunette holding her head in her hands as if jealous of the stream of females from his horn.

"One of ours," said Andrzej. "Rzupinski. An old friend of—" He jerked his head disrespectfully at the kitchen and winked. "Friend of mine, too, until I stopped feeding him. Like an animal in the zoo, eh? But he plays like a lion."

He reverently uncovered a turntable that looked assembled from the spare parts of several. I was sure—though she later denied it—that the jealous woman on the record cover was Maja. I glanced down the titles of the tunes, given in Polish ("Milowe Kroki") and, parenthetically, English.

Straight rhythm section, drums, bass, piano, all new to me, plus Rzupinski. Recorded ten years earlier.

"What's your groove?" said Andrzej soberly.

"Try 'Giant Steps.' "

This tune is one of the most perilous in modern jazz. Written by John Coltrane as a kind of test flight for his harmonic ideas, expanded from one challenging section of a well-known standard, it is a minefield for improvisers. The tune changes key radically every two bars, meaning every one and a half seconds at a high tempo. Every serious saxophonist learns his way around Trane's superb solo, but few risk putting out their own version. I'd worked on "Giant Steps" for years, but rarely played it in public—alongside Coltrane's tenor roar, any clarinet attempt sounds pipsqueak.

It impressed me that Rzupinski had dared to record it. "Giant Steps" is Everest; to fall from its heights is to fall to your doom, and believe me, everyone can tell. Though I've heard numerous horn players take it to the limit in public, when the red light goes on in the recording booth and the microphone is open, and there's none of the human darkness, fever, and adrenal concentration of a club, but only you and the tape rolling—or you and John Coltrane's long shadow—what genuine musical experience is likely to come out of such an occasion?

"I don't remember this record so well," said Andrzej. "A funny thing. Fellow comes round your flat a couple of times a week, you listen to his music, you play it when people visit. You design a great album cover, he feels proud, you feel proud. Then you break apart your friendship, suddenly you never want to hear another note."

I imagined many vodka gatherings, long winter nights and not so many records and always a bad needle on a makeshift stereo.

He waved to his wife. "Say, what happened to the vodka? Where the hell are we, Cameroon? Give this man a glass of the national symbol and let him get started."

He preened his ponytail in irritation and sat upright, a Buddha among the records scattered on the floor, as the first scratchings of the disc came on. I leaned back in the sofa and tried to second-guess a young Rzupinski. Since he dared to do the tune, it must be at a frenetic, youthful tempo, surely.

Not at all: it began nobly, elegiacally, the melody intoned like a vast, slow hymn, carefully pronounced and ever so slightly altered to give it a majestic bearing. As a melody "Giant Steps" can sound a little rickety, too much an excuse for the unusual harmonies that support it, but Rzupinski gave it an enormous warmth and timbre, that humane sound you still hear in the great Cuban players.

So he was taking a surprise approach. My own trick was often to take one of those Charlie Parker tunes—intricate bebop melodies that all sound cut from the same cloth—and play them a bit slower than anyone expects, for then they reveal a hidden grace and delight they lose when you try to race through them in order to prove that, gee whiz, you know what you're doing.

Rzupinski's second slow, more elaborate statement of the melody closed in silence. I was just about to comment approvingly on what an unusual strategy he'd taken when suddenly the rhythm section kicked in, very fast, and Rzupinski attacked. He came swooping in like a bomber strafing a burning city. I found myself gripping the sofa arm as he soared through that encircling maze of harmonies with unleashed fury. I could only gape at the young man's passion and speed, his astonishing command. He was a true virtuoso, and I'd never heard anyone in the jazz community in the West admit how extraordinary he was.

The solo ended in a blaze of glory, an intricate cadenza on the penultimate chord that took the whole tune into account, and when the final piano crash reverberated into the scratching silence, Andrzej took the needle off and said matter-of-factly, "Too much, eh? Guess what, I found Louis."

Maja came out of the kitchen with Andrzej's wife. She said, "I was in the studio when he recorded that. You remember what I told you about how he used to practice?"

"These goddamned women," said Andrzej to me, as "St. James Infirmary" came on, Armstrong ripsnorting in Russia, our sincerest ambassador. "They think they're responsible because they happen to be in the same room. Man, we know better."

"You don't think inspiration is a real force?" said Maja. "Seriously? I think it's a more important force than politics, or sex, or hunger. Or anything but love. Because you can't refuse it. It asks for what it wants, and no matter what you try it doesn't listen to no as your answer."

"Maybe it sometimes comes with love," said Andrzej's wife. She had the look of a devoted schoolteacher, a woman smart enough to handle her husband. She seemed content to have Maja as ally rather than rival.

"And in America?" said Andrzej. "I understand they spend millions of dollars on the study of inspiration and the chemical analysis of inspiration and the inspiration of inspiration. Always the encouragement of inspiration. Isn't that so?"

I said, "You'd be surprised. We spend more money on military bands than all the other kinds of inspiration put together. That's the kind of encouragement my government likes. A good parade."

"I like this guy," said Andrzej to Maja. "I don't understand him, but I like his politics. Are we agreed, then, that women only inspire love? That art and cathedrals come from man and God, and jazz is still the devil's music? I hope so, man." He drained his glass of vodka and yelled, "*Na zdrowie!*" He calmed. "Good to be among old friends." He addressed Maja with a salutary glint in his eyes. "By the way, I'm writing my memoirs at last."

"Again?" she asked.

The wife said something in Polish to Maja and they both laughed.

"Fuck your conspiracy," said Andrzej. "Not *again*. For the last time. You're not going to be in it, by the way."

"I'm relieved," said Maja. "I don't want to be in anyone's memoirs. It makes me depressed to hear you even talking about them. Wait until you're an old man, no? When a man is too tired to invent, then he writes his memoirs."

"I don't invent. I tell the truth. Truth in Poland is almost unheard of," he said to me. "You know why? Because Poles can't agree on anything. They feel they're having their pockets picked when they give in. They can't even agree on what's on the record player in front of them. If there were four authentic Polacks here they'd be fighting over which sax player Rzupinski paid to make that record for him."

I said something about his posters. I'd decided they couldn't be stashed in this apartment; Maja had estimated several thousand, collected over the decades.

He shook his head. Louis was singing now—"Mandy, Make Up Your Mind."

"I sold them," he said quietly, and lifted his empty glass.

"What?" said Maja.

"To leave this flat," said his wife.

"But you own this flat since—" said Maja.

"I thought I'd give the flat to my mother," said Andrzej.

"Too many bills and we have only a little money. I imagined I could sell the collection, pay everyone, and leave." He shrugged. "I got less than I thought. I found a dealer in Vienna who would give me a good price, right? Impossible. The government doesn't give me permission to export the posters. You remember how many there are. They don't even give me papers to export my own originals. Suppose everyone does it? they say. Like there are dozens of me. So what choice do I have? I sold them to an official in the Ministry of Education. He agreed to find me a permanent teaching position next year, and I got my money in dollars. We still have the bloody flat, but no worries. For the first time. Now I can write my memoirs in peace."

"You sold your posters to write your memoirs?" said Maja with a nervous laugh.

"It seemed a good idea," said his wife. "You see, it's a fact, now. It's impossible for us both to find work at the same time. So we have a kind of insurance in the bank."

"But you were going to leave," said Maja. "How much did you get?"

"Enough."

"But not enough to leave?"

"Yes, goddamn you. What am I going to leave for? What shall I do when I get to bloody London? Teach Polish to little British crumpets? Teach English to bloody Polish emigrés? I'd rather stay here." He turned to me. "What do you think? I did the only right thing, no?"

I said, "If you feel this is a home you can never leave."

"It is my home, and it doesn't feel like my home, but anyway, I can't turn my back. Maybe I will call my memoirs this. *When My Back Was Turned.* Anyway, it's where we collect our mail. It's where I keep my Louis Armstrong collection. You think there's any market in America for my memoirs?"

"Not if you leave out the best parts," said his wife drily. We all laughed, a little uncomfortable.

"That's the trouble with inspiration, you see," said Andrzej, holding out his glass to be refilled. "Even if you discourage it, inspiration keeps coming back for more. And it always believes a little beauty is worth a lot of punishment."

"There are some important things I must tell you," Maja said. "I don't want you to make wrong conclusions from last night. When I was in too much of a dancing mood."

Along the forested edge of Lake Stilton the water was ablaze with afternoon sunlight, a couple of sails diverging across the ruffled surface. Though the lake was only a mile wide, as we walked around it along the single road, the hotel and the town began to seem far enough away for me to feel alone with her.

In a moment, I thought, no matter what she says, everything will begin again.

"I can feel what you're thinking," she said. "Everyone can see us here."

"They've all got binoculars?"

"Simon does," she said. "And his windows at the hotel are on this side."

The spy across the street, the secret police under the bed.

"He likes that he can watch the sails," she said. "One day he wants to buy an old boat and repair it so we can visit the Pacific islands. I think he's the only man I've met who loves travel as much as I do."

I was tempted to dispute her claim. We'd walked nearly halfway around the lake, watching the sky go overcast. Quite rapidly the air grew heavy, sultry; it would rain soon, Maja said.

As we started back she suggested we have tea at the little house she shared with Simon, we could do our important talking there. I wondered hopefully if that hadn't always been part of the afternoon's plan.

"You should know," she said, "when a Polack invites you in for tea, you can't refuse. And if a Polack doesn't ask you in for tea, that means you've done something terrible. This would never happen, I hope."

"So everyone's drinking tea all the time in Poland?"

"And vodka."

"What happens if I refuse?"

"I never speak with you again," she said merrily. "And I've changed my mind. I'm thinking you remind me of someone in Gombrowicz instead. You haven't read him? Polish. He lived in Argentina. Beautiful writer, a bit crazy. Maybe," she finished, "one day I should end up also in Buenos Aires."

She pronounced it with an exotic accent that was all wrong, but I didn't correct her. This was pure Maja: preoccupied with a problem close at hand, her conversation leaped across the globe, as if speaking of distant climes cleared the air.

The little house they shared was down the first of the rough side lanes in the town, a cottage in someone else's back garden, past prodigious sunflowers and a vegetable patch. It was cluttered with the anonymous possessions of people who don't stay more than a couple of years in one place. Paperbacks, T-shirts, an art museum poster or two; a few local baskets that would be jettisoned when they moved on; warm-weather furniture that belonged to the cottage. If they had to, I thought, they could pack in an hour.

Flowers stood in drinking glasses around the all-purpose room. A few snapshots of Maja, alone or with Simon, usually on a beach somewhere. In one she stood in snow, a little younger, before a medieval castle.

I held it up—she was in the kitchen area. "Poland?"

She squinted. "Snow? It must be. Your town, Cracow."

I replaced it. "I've been trying to get gigs in Eastern Europe for years. Sometimes there's work for foreign musicians, but it's almost impossible to arrange from the States." I added, as much for myself as for her, "I've got to get a European booking agent one of these days."

"You want to give concerts in Poland?" she called out.

"Can you help me?"

"I can try. You won't gain much money, though."

"That doesn't matter."

She said, "But you mustn't ever sell yourself for too little. This is always the Polish way. I know too many musicians who always did this and then they never stop. If you know how good you are, you must ask for what you hope to get. Because no one offers if you don't ask. I've learned this a hundred times."

Everyone understands the music business except professional musicians, of course. Still, I was touched that she was trying to protect me.

There was also a prominent photo of a little blue-sweatered boy with golden hair, six or seven, with his hands pressed against a rough stone wall behind him, happily pushing against it. He was astonishingly pretty—there is no other word. Simon's son by Maja's predecessor, perhaps.

Was he here? Could he be here? I glanced around while Maja fiddled with the kettle. No small clothes lying anywhere, no toys scattered, no children's books poking out of the paperbacks.

"What a beautiful boy. Who is he?"

Maja said, "That's my son, Benjamin."

She was smiling like a magician, as if she'd just announced nothing behind her back, nothing up her sleeve, then presto!

I managed to ask, "Where is he?"

"In Amsterdam."

"With his father?"

"His father's back in Poland."

"Rzupinski?"

She looked aghast. "Are you a lunatic?"

"Sorry."

She recovered. "No, no. But he is a musician. An electric guitarist. One of the best in Poland. You see, I always end up with musicians. I don't know why, they're not responsible people."

"Some of us are."

She said, "Perhaps because they know you cannot trust words. And they find another way to say everything just as precise." She added a bit nervously, "You're surprised about Benjamin, aren't you. Why?"

Because, I thought, your body doesn't look as if it's given birth. Because you seemed complete, but I see I was only meeting half of you.

She said, "Since nearly three weeks he stays with my best friend in A'dam." A teapot clanked in her hands. "Too long."

She set two mugs of tea across the table from each other,

steaming domestically. Even in summer, this far south the weather could be unpredictable in mid-afternoon, in a breezy cottage in the shade of trees.

"You were very young when he was born," I said.

She thought back. "Twenty-four. Is that so young? Benjamin's father and I weren't together for long. But he's a very intelligent man and a sweet man. I was pregnant by accident, and then I thought, Why not have a child now? When he's grown up, I won't be old."

"It must've been difficult to leave Poland with him."

I was trying to place the boy in the context of what little I knew—the sleeping on friends' sofas.

"It could've been worse. I got out, I got Benjamin out. He has a good school now and will get a Dutch passport this year."

I realized then that the difficulty hadn't been leaving Poland, but getting another country to take them in officially. Strange: I'd been flirting with two lives, not one.

She was watching my face carefully. She said, "Look, I have to speak to you honestly. I didn't tell you about him because what was the point? At first I thought you were just another man trying to pull me on the beach, and I don't have to explain myself to you. Then I realized we would be friends. Perhaps not the kind that seems natural to you and to me, but never mind."

I said, "I don't understand what you're doing here."

She waited.

I said, "You seem suffocated here."

"I don't understand."

"Bored." Actually, she seemed tortured.

She said, "No one can be bored when there's a possibility to change. In Poland I was bored. Here—" She glanced involuntarily around at the life she was in the process of choosing. "Here I'm trying to decide what's best for Benjamin and me."

"You've been considering this a long time?"

"It's been difficult with Simon for more than a year. Since he decides to leave Holland. He wanted me to come with him then. But I was sure it was already over. I wanted him to go. Then I begin to miss him. I don't meet anyone else who interests me at all. He keeps telephoning, writing, asking me to come marry him. He said it went badly in Amsterdam when we were all together because we weren't serious. And so I should come by myself. Even just for a short time, to see." She halted abruptly and clasped her hands on the table.

Three lives, rather.

"I said we should wait until the summer to try. So Benjamin and I can come for a few months, both of us. Benjamin was already back in his school in A'dam, you see. But Simon said that was too long to wait to find out." She paused. "My friend who watches him is Polish also. With a girl in the same class."

"I don't understand. Couldn't Benjamin go to school here now? So you could both stay longer, to see how it worked?"

"I said this also. But Simon said they don't take him into the school here in the middle of everything for just a month or two. And anyway, Benjamin is habituated to lessons in Dutch. His English is good but he would have to stay behind one year. A different system or something. Simon thought it wasn't a good idea, he wants us to decide when it's just the two of us."

"Simon didn't want him to come?"

She said edgily, "Simon had a very English childhood. He went away to school when he was younger than Benjamin. It doesn't seem so difficult to him that I should be away for a few weeks. He thinks I'm being the sensitive mother."

Suffocated was right, after all. Was she really convinced she had a future with a man who talked her out of bringing her son?

"So are you going to marry him?"

She said testily, "I don't know. I have Benjamin, I don't have anything else. I don't have a country, I don't have a work I love, I don't have a flat I care about. And Simon is ready to look after us. Maybe he's not the perfect man in the world for me, but this isn't so important as it was a few years ago. It would be very good for Benjamin to be around him again, they get along. But I'm not sure if I'm ready to join Simon again for a few months or for a year or forever. Or how long I can play chess with myself. And only read and walk Benjamin to school in this boring town by the pretty lake. All I try to find out since I left Poland is why the moments I want to find in my life haven't happened, is it because of me or perhaps it's no one's fault."

No wonder she wanted to take back what she'd said last night. I could feel her relief at having told me all this—having put me at arm's length—but in her voice I also heard frustration and surrender. I was astonished at how angry I felt on her behalf. What was this experiment Simon had forced her into? What could a month without her son settle of her problems with this man, except make Maja feel guilty and the boy feel left out? And that crap about the schools—as if they couldn't have waited another month for the boy's vacation. It sounded as if Simon was only trying to polish his own third-rate gig at this dinky tourist settlement. Meanwhile, Maja's life with her son in Amsterdam, job and all, got suitably derailed.

She said, "You must not think only because you see me here like this that I don't have many things I want to do.

I was studying photography at a very good program in A'dam. It's something I see for myself in the future, I can see I have a talent."

I said, "You must miss your son terribly. I'm sure it's expensive to call Holland."

She poured me more tea and a full mug for herself—it gave her hands some release. "I write him letters. Twice a week. It's not for much longer. Then we see what we do."

I had the uncanny sensation that she wanted me to grab her by the shoulders and shake her, talk her out of it. Why else was she saying all this? Not simply to stop me from going after her; there were easier ways. To persuade me into going ahead no matter what she told me, perhaps.

I said—playing devil's advocate with myself—"You and Simon have been happy together, though."

"For a couple of years it seemed natural to be with him," said Maja. "We made many small travels around Europe. To Greece, to Ibiza, to Tunisia. We took Benjamin everywhere. Like an easy adventure. And I know I can trust Simon absolutely. But then he begins to think he must do better, he can't earn more in Amsterdam, and perhaps it will be best professionally if he returns to New Zealand. And somewhere it stops being like an easy adventure between us and becomes instead like—like the long afternoon at school in the hot weather when you're a child." She shook her head. "I shouldn't be telling you these things."

"It's none of my business, I know."

"I didn't mean that. I'm afraid you'll believe I am the most difficult woman in the world. But if things don't go well, it's better for everyone to try something else, don't you think?"

She was staring at me with her whole soul in her eyes, asking me to convince her that she didn't belong anymore

---

——— (WARSAW)

We tried to be back in Lena's flat by five each evening, when it grew dark and the enormous and ugly Palace of Culture loomed larger than ever, blotting out half the lights of the city with its shadow—like an Evil Empire State Building. Snow fell fitfully, and it was a relief to enter Lena's apartment, overheated but spacious and at ease above all the deprivation below. I was trying to buy a shirt for Maja's father for Christmas. I'd met him briefly when he stopped by to give her money: a tall, iron-jawed, bristly-haired man who acted as if he'd seen his daughter only a week ago and not the year before last. He spoke no English.

There were no shirts anywhere. Or rather there were three: a green, a white, a light blue, all badly made, with tapered collars, and available in three sizes, pile upon pile, in shop after shop. I felt stupid for not having bought in with this man, and might eventually be free to belong to someone else.

She said, "I'd like to come by your room tomorrow afternoon. For a concert. I must hear you play before you leave."

"All right."

"No misunderstandings?"

"No misunderstandings. Bring anyone else you like."

She sighed. "I wish Benjamin could hear you. He's mad to play the flute. I think he would like the clarinet as much. He says he sees fantastic pictures when he hears music."

For an instant I had a flash of the eight-year-old I'd been: practicing for hours in my father's basement workshop so as not to disturb the parents and older sister upstairs. Funny, that basement (ideal acoustics, perfectly dry in winter) had got me to this lake on the other side of the world.

"You ought to get him started on an instrument soon."

"I will. When I go back. Even if he and I return here."

Speaking about her son illuminated her, altered the air around her.

I said, "Did you ever show Simon your country?"

"Never. You know, Poland doesn't sound so interesting when you're always meeting people who feel extremely lucky they left."

At that moment, I knew that the more time I spent with Maja, even in another man's cottage, the more I would want to plunge into her and her contradictions and problems. I needed to regroup and catch my breath; to give her my address in New York, leave, and let ten thousand miles blow away a flirtation that should probably never have begun in the first place.

I thought this and thought simultaneously how very natural it felt to be around her.

"Do you know Amsterdam?" she asked.

"I was there once, a few years ago. Passing through."

"You should have called me." She closed her eyes sleepily. "Do you think we would have made love?"

I fumbled at a reply.

She carried the teapot to the sink, emptied its remnants, looked over at me. She grinned. "Fantastic pictures, eh?"

We didn't kiss good-bye, though.

I was studying photography at a very good program in A'dam. It's something I see for myself in the future, I can see I have a talent."

I said, "You must miss your son terribly. I'm sure it's expensive to call Holland."

She poured me more tea and a full mug for herself—it gave her hands some release. "I write him letters. Twice a week. It's not for much longer. Then we see what we do."

I had the uncanny sensation that she wanted me to grab her by the shoulders and shake her, talk her out of it. Why else was she saying all this? Not simply to stop me from going after her; there were easier ways. To persuade me into going ahead no matter what she told me, perhaps.

I said—playing devil's advocate with myself—"You and Simon have been happy together, though."

"For a couple of years it seemed natural to be with him," said Maja. "We made many small travels around Europe. To Greece, to Ibiza, to Tunisia. We took Benjamin everywhere. Like an easy adventure. And I know I can trust Simon absolutely. But then he begins to think he must do better, he can't earn more in Amsterdam, and perhaps it will be best professionally if he returns to New Zealand. And somewhere it stops being like an easy adventure between us and becomes instead like—like the long afternoon at school in the hot weather when you're a child." She shook her head. "I shouldn't be telling you these things."

"It's none of my business, I know."

"I didn't mean that. I'm afraid you'll believe I am the most difficult woman in the world. But if things don't go well, it's better for everyone to try something else, don't you think?"

She was staring at me with her whole soul in her eyes, asking me to convince her that she didn't belong anymore with this man, and might eventually be free to belong to someone else.

She said, "I'd like to come by your room tomorrow afternoon. For a concert. I must hear you play before you leave."

"All right."

"No misunderstandings?"

"No misunderstandings. Bring anyone else you like."

She sighed. "I wish Benjamin could hear you. He's mad to play the flute. I think he would like the clarinet as much. He says he sees fantastic pictures when he hears music."

For an instant I had a flash of the eight-year-old I'd been: practicing for hours in my father's basement workshop so as not to disturb the parents and older sister upstairs. Funny, that basement (ideal acoustics, perfectly dry in winter) had got me to this lake on the other side of the world.

"You ought to get him started on an instrument soon."

"I will. When I go back. Even if he and I return here."

Speaking about her son illuminated her, altered the air around her.

I said, "Did you ever show Simon your country?"

"Never. You know, Poland doesn't sound so interesting when you're always meeting people who feel extremely lucky they left."

At that moment, I knew that the more time I spent with Maja, even in another man's cottage, the more I would want to plunge into her and her contradictions and problems. I needed to regroup and catch my breath; to give her my address in New York, leave, and let ten thousand miles blow away a flirtation that should probably never have begun in the first place.

I thought this and thought simultaneously how very natural it felt to be around her.

"Do you know Amsterdam?" she asked.

"I was there once, a few years ago. Passing through."

"You should have called me." She closed her eyes sleepily. "Do you think we would have made love?"

I fumbled at a reply.

She carried the teapot to the sink, emptied its remnants, looked over at me. She grinned. "Fantastic pictures, eh?"

We didn't kiss good-bye, though.

———————— (W A R S A W)

We tried to be back in Lena's flat by five each evening, when it grew dark and the enormous and ugly Palace of Culture loomed larger than ever, blotting out half the lights of the city with its shadow—like an Evil Empire State Building. Snow fell fitfully, and it was a relief to enter Lena's apartment, overheated but spacious and at ease above all the deprivation below. I was trying to buy a shirt for Maja's father for Christmas. I'd met him briefly when he stopped by to give her money: a tall, iron-jawed, bristly-haired man who acted as if he'd seen his daughter only a week ago and not the year before last. He spoke no English.

There were no shirts anywhere. Or rather there were three: a green, a white, a light blue, all badly made, with tapered collars, and available in three sizes, pile upon pile, in shop after shop. I felt stupid for not having bought in

Amsterdam when I'd had the chance. And what gift here could possibly interest Lena?

I couldn't grasp Maja's relation with her. Lena seemed to give the orders, and she was putting us up for two weeks, but every day she went out alone with string bags and came back fully laden from the market without a complaint. She did let me give her money for the food, though.

By five-thirty the supplies—fresh dark bread, white cheese, several salamis—were laid out on wooden slabs, the first tea drunk, internal warmth restored. By six people began to arrive. To come for tea in the early evening and stay for supper (with luck, a stew) was a ritual, and neither Lena nor Maja seemed surprised at whoever or how many showed up, often without calling. The telephone system was labyrinthine: sometimes the only way to communicate across Warsaw was to call whichever was this week's magic village on the other side of Poland and get them to patch you through.

Those social evenings were exhausting. I understood practically nothing of what was said, though I knew I was being scrutinized to see if I measured up to their idea of what an American should be. Yet they were careful to show a total lack of interest, even a contempt, for most things American. I took this as a backhanded compliment. I could see how crazy they were for cassettes, and jeans, and how successfully Maja recounted her visits to New York. I was a reminder of all they were missing: someone forced to slither through the fists of bureacracy all his life had every reason to resent my currency and my blithe passport. I never met a Pole who believed an American could have any problems worth taking seriously—I suppose this is their revenge for knowing we regard them as threadbare and deeply incompetent. It is an insurmountable barrier to friendship, not accepting that the other person can have difficulties too.

Most of Lena's friends were younger. There was Zosia, a small dark-haired beauty who seemed to have Asian or Spanish blood in her; Ulrik, a swaggering barrel-chested fellow who was forever downing shots of vodka, which he brought and poured himself; a skinny bald guy with a straggly beard who was a literature professor and remained skeptically silent and drank more than Ulrik; Magda, rather plain, who always helped in the kitchen, wasn't afraid to try her English on me, and whose husband was up in Gdansk all week for his office; Wojciech the poet; and a dozen others who came and went, smoking and drinking and talking nonstop. It struck me as an Eastern European version of Dublin, but they saw themselves as Parisian, sophisticated in their high style and clever talk, their constant smoking.

The irony, of course, was that these proud young people were ten to twenty years out of step. The women still dressed like hippies, and when they were trying to be elegant, it was without restraint and mismatched, as if they simply wore as much as they could. The men tried to look like bearded beatnik revolutionaries, which I guess they authentically were. For people with such a haphazard connection to the outside world they were confident in their pronouncements. Not about politics, which they could take in via the BBC World Service or the Voice of America, but on whatever was the latest wave in, say, Rome or Los Angeles. They were so out of touch they had no idea how out of touch they were. They did realize that on Park Avenue or in Soho now it was hip, it was stylish, it was politically fashionable to be Polish.

They had two television channels for several hours every evening, though one ceased functioning for days while I was there. People would gather around Lena's television, and a sort of competition ensued to see who could make the wittiest insulting remarks during the newscast. Since there was nothing entertaining on TV, this became their entertainment. They would feed on the nightly serving of government propaganda and regurgitate it to amuse themselves. A century ago Americans gathered around the family piano and sang along; here they collected around the heavyset Russian TV and talked back and drowned it out.

They took themselves very seriously, for I rarely saw one of these Poles make fun of himself—eight centuries of struggle for churches, farms, and dockyards tends to direct people's sense of humor outward. Instead they always seemed to be making pointed jokes about each other (I had the impression every Pole could read his neighbor instantly) or about "the situation," laughing sardonically in the face of impossibility and gloom. Perhaps the ability to make fun of oneself only comes when desperation goes? They hadn't been able to do much to contradict the larger situation of martial law, so instead they'd learned to pass the time by contradicting each other.

"Ever since I can remember," said Maja, "it's always been like this. Not only since martial law. In Poland everyone is always in trouble with everyone else. Don't you enjoy it?"

In morning light Warsaw's well-preserved town square looked as elegant and unconvincing as a stage set for a Mozart opera. Its sunstruck houses, four centuries old, all had statuesque figures, ships and faces and wreaths and coats of arms carved or painted on pastry facades of gray or lavender, yellow or brown, outlined in white icing. Each house on the flagstoned square had a steep red-tiled roof, an arched black door, and a little ground-floor shop, its windows full of stamps or souvenir books or carved saints for the few foreign tourists gaping at such unexpected beauty. A couple of watercolor painters stamped their feet before identical displays. In several restaurants lamps already glowed behind thin curtains.

"The Rynek," said Maja. "I wanted to show it to you for months now. What do you think?"

The day was frigid but dry; I can't recall now which of the early days it was, though the French friends of Lena's certainly hadn't arrived yet at the flat. Soldiers, as always, were everywhere, gawky in their squat fur hats and long green coats. I was surprised at first that Maja greeted them, or responded to their nods, but then nearly everyone had been a soldier at some point.

"The houses aren't old, you know," said Maja. "The square looks real, but it's new."

"You're kidding."

"I'll show you photographs. The Nazis destroyed the square completely and we rebuilt it after the war. To the original plans, eh? We looked at paintings from centuries back, like Canaletto, and put the real bricks back like a puzzle. Or we copied the old ones. Even the streets." She kicked the cobblestones with her boot. "We had to put it all together from nothing. Nothing was standing."

It was finally dawning on me that though they might loathe and make fun of the Soviets, they still hated, really hated, the Nazis.

Because of the approaching holiday, all Warsaw was out walking, even in the bitter cold, and the square had a festive humor that I guessed it must lose immediately in January. No one seemed to mind the stiffening breeze off the nearby river; people walked with leisure, their faces and hands exposed, and the soda-water vendors still kept up a brisk business.

I saw the most beautiful girls, stylish and assured blue-eyed princesses with long hair, walking alongside the most improbably sloppy young men—shabby, defensive, and exasperated. The old men had less frustrated faces, and a resilience in their glance; Polish women over forty looked bitten by worry, with careworn mouths and heavy-lidded eyes.

"One of these coffeehouses," said Maja, "had jazz in the evenings. Years ago. I can ask. We can come to hear it, if you like."

"That's why I brought my horn," I said. "I hope we can find Rzupinski."

"The first thing he'll try to do is borrow money from you, you know."

"I'd still like to meet him."

Off the old square, on a narrow cobblestoned street where Maja remembered a sympathetic coffeehouse, a long queue of mostly men, standing sullenly and exhaling frosted breath like tired horses, stretched around the corner from a shop.

"What are they waiting for?"

She grinned. "Vodka, of course. They buy it for friends for Christmas. Then they drink it themselves."

Even for that they had to wait in line.

In the café we sat beside a lace-curtained front window, away from the fire. We had the wood-beamed room to ourselves except for a few students at a table in the back— "preparing for their Christmas examinations," said Maja.

With Maja in her own country at last, after hearing about it for months, I should've felt fulfilled, not disappointed. Perhaps it was my fault: I didn't speak the language, and I was still tired after a month of closing down my flat to come join her in Amsterdam.

I asked, "Do I look worn out to you?"

"You look better than in New York. You were pale there. You were gray. Now you look a little cold. But very healthy."

"I left exactly one week ago," I said.

"Only one week? It seems longer, no?"

"I was wondering," I said, "if you were sparing me at night because you thought I needed rest."

She said, "I can't do something unless I feel it."

She glanced out at the square for a moment.

I said, "It must be a bit strange for you to be here after a couple of years away. I hope you're not uneasy because I came with you."

"Poland always feels strange to me," she said. "That's not because of you. But anyway, I warned you two months ago. Over the telephone."

"I don't remember."

"We were speaking of when you might join me in A'dam. I said to hurry over the Atlantic right away. In an hour. For dinner. And you didn't come."

"We were talking about whether you might visit New York for a week," I said. "Because I was so delayed. I thought you were joking."

"Did you think it was so funny, what I said?"

"I thought you couldn't be serious."

She shrugged. "It's a mystery, no? Maybe you should speak to one of those beautiful Polish girls everywhere around. They're twenty, very friendly. Not difficult like me."

"Perhaps I should. This isn't the issue."

"Perhaps," she said, turning my own word on me. "Anyway, I have to leave. I promised Benjamin I'd get him at my mother's and we all go to Lazienki Park. Do you want to join us?"

"If you'd like me to."

She grimaced. "I don't know how you decide which notes to play."

"I play what I hear," I said. "If I hear it wrong, I play it wrong."

_____(PORT STILTON)

I'm not trying to blame Maja for all that happened. It was I who in only a few days seduced myself into the idea of her; I who later grew obsessed, from the other side of the world, with her predicament, her body, her possibility. And I who fell in love with the obsession. Still, how could I have been so willing to shape my life around—what? Not the wrong woman: that presupposes a right woman. The wrong notes in myself?

But as somebody said, jazz is making the wrong notes sound right.

And if it comes down to a choice, rather than parceling out blame, I'd much rather be convinced that Maja was simply an inevitable accident. Not one of many, the sort of woman I should avoid, but rather a kind of female Halley's Comet, a fiery wanderer who comes along once in a lifetime, trailing only sparks, not omens.

That next New Zealand morning I was sitting in a rattan

armchair, sipping the dregs of breakfast tea—room-service tray at my feet, towel wrapped around my waist—when the door opened and in shot Halley's Comet, ablaze, aloft, alone.

She was in her beach outfit of green shorts and a black bikini top. "I came to see if the concert could start early," she said.

I got up to kiss her.

She gave me her cheek. "No misunderstandings, remember?" she said warmly. She perched on the edge of the bed. "Do you mind playing for me now instead? I forgot that today is Simon's afternoon free."

Either he wasn't interested in hearing me, or she'd decided she wanted us to be alone. My instrument case was already out and open.

I said, "Start with a little Mozart."

"Aren't you going to put on your clothes first?"

"Why?"

"You're not properly dressed for Mozart."

"Try reading his biography."

After all, it was my hotel room. And she hadn't knocked. Plus it was my clarinet.

She said, "I'm serious, it's disturbing. And what if the maid comes in? It wasn't easy to get here with no one seeing me."

Now I was sure she hadn't told Simon she was coming. With all the hope in the world, I cracked the door, hung out the leave-me-alone sign, and locked out the invisible crowd.

When I came out of the bathroom, having pulled on some shorts and a T-shirt, she'd already slipped out of her sandals and tucked her long legs under her on the bed.

Standing before the window, basking in sunlight, gradually warming up, I gave her the Mozart quintet first movement, two short Bach transcriptions, and part of a gorgeous Milhaud sonata accessible even to people who hate the twentieth century.

Maja listened with complete attention; she could transfix you in an electrical current of concentration. Nothing could've been more compelling to me than the way she half lay with her eyes closed and her legs stretched out on my bed, following every gesture of the music. One bare foot gently keeping time, holding back when I did, following my phrasing.

I thought: This woman must be a wonderful lover.

To round off the recital I improvised a free version of "Someone to Watch Over Me." I was surprised to find myself feeling slightly nervous, but I always have a superb tone and that's what, at the end of the day, a non-musician hears most.

As I cleaned and dismantled the instrument and put it away, she said, "You know, you're very lucky to have something to do well all your life. To improve at. And you carry it around with you. When I danced I knew it was only for a time, that at a certain moment I would never be better. That's why I stopped." She got off the bed to watch what I was doing. "Maybe that's why I still pay attention to chess. To have something to do a little better every year. But there isn't so much beauty in chess."

"Even to a great player?"

"That kind of solving problems isn't beauty to me. I can't bear formal beauty. If you'd lived for years with Stalinist architecture you'd feel the same, believe me. I'd rather look at a few beach chairs."

"We might as well go for a swim, then."

"That's a good idea."

"Unless you'd like to get undressed."

She said softly, "Perhaps we get a chance to make love

in another country one day. We won't make love in this country."

I said, "What if my plane crashes? Or you get married here and we never see each other again?"

She said seriously, almost disconsolately, "*I* don't know what to do either. I'm not playing games with you. You're the one who might only be playing games with me, eh?"

"I promise you, no." So seriously that I surprised myself, I added, "Listen to me. We must see each other again. I've never met anybody like you."

She said, "You can't meet everyone, you know. Have you forgotten I have a little boy? That I love very dearly and who is always with me? You see, you haven't met me, really, because you haven't met him. He's a wonderful, very sweet, very smart boy. And Benjamin goes where I go. I would never do again what I've done this month. Never, never. So I don't know what you see for us in any future."

"Look," I said. "To start with, I would never ask you or anyone else to do that. And I see that you don't have a future with a man who doesn't want your son around."

She said quietly. "But for you and me, right now all I see, honestly, is a plane ticket that passes through Los Angeles. And I know Benjamin is waiting for me at the other end."

She wanted to see if I would back down.

I said, "I get to Europe all the time."

She went to the open window. She didn't lean out, but put her elbows on the sill, her head back so no one below could spot her. She said offhandedly, "You still haven't let me play you at chess. You're afraid of losing. I'm beginning to think you don't even know how to play."

I came up behind her, as I assumed she wanted, slid my fingers under the elastic waistband of her shorts, and in one go pulled them down to her ankles; obediently she stepped out of them. Her scrap of black bikini made her seem nearly naked, leaning forward against the window sill, her legs tightly joined. In morning heat she had the perfection of a peeled peach, glossy and smooth-skinned, with the hint of a leaf protruding at the split.

She didn't budge from the window. I put my hands across her bare stomach and pulled her to me. She said into my shoulder, "Don't move, hold me there."

She was grimacing, biting her lower lip.

"Someone looks up at the window," she murmured.

"It looks like we're having a normal conversation."

My hands began to roam her, up and gently around.

"No, *no.*" In an instant she'd moved away from me and pushed her hair back behind her ears. "What a compliment," she said, and grinned down at me. She said, "You squeeze too hard. You left finger-marks all over me."

"I'm sorry." I didn't see what she was talking about.

"I shouldn't have asked you to play for me. The trouble is, I trust my ears. You should play less well."

"Thank you."

"It's good you're leaving," she said firmly.

"You should travel in my suitcase."

She said, "Don't joke when it's important."

What a tremendous thing it is, to watch a beautiful woman dress.

"I'm not joking."

Reed player to the rescue.

She gazed at me curiously. "I have a better idea. We will go to the beach in front of the hotel, where everyone can see us. And I will let you win the first chess game, just to warm the teapot, you see? And perhaps even the second game. I'll make some very naive moves. You'll put a little more money down each time. And then—" She grinned. "Checkmate, my friend. And I'll have my plane ticket."

"Via New York?"

"Via Buenos Aires."

I went in the bathroom to put on my swim trunks— scrupulously observing her boundaries.

"What about dinner tonight?" I asked after I'd changed.

"Simon and I are invited to the hotel manager's house for dinner. That's his uncle. He has to go. So I must go."

"His uncle? I suppose his father owns the hotel."

"That's the other uncle," she said. "And a big hotel in Christchurch, too."

"Now I understand."

She said, "Simon wants us to have dinner tomorrow night. The three of us."

"Why on earth does he want that?"

I could've said simply *no*.

"It's normal, isn't it?"

"Won't he suspect something, if he doesn't already?"

"I don't know what he should suspect. And you should not be the one uncomfortable. You're leaving, I'm the one who's staying."

"I'd rather have dinner with you alone, my last night. It'll seem strange to have him there."

She said, "Stranger for me than for you, I promise."

We spoke now as if my bags were already packed: my parting stood like a wall of black water between us.

"Simon told me he has a bad instinct about you," she said. "He warns that I should not believe everything you say."

I protested briefly about my trustworthiness, fine up-standing character, etcetera. I must've sounded like a fif-teen-year-old.

"There's nothing more fascinating than someone you're not sure of, eh?" she said. "You might change your mind about me if you know me more."

"I hope not."

"Of course," she said, "I would like us to fall in love with each other forever. Whether we see each other again or not. Oh, I didn't tell you—I asked about planes at the travel agent's this morning. I can make a small stopover in New York if I want."

I did not say what was almost in me to say. Instead we went down to the blank beach. Her play proved confident, careful, and very strong. The sky was bald and hot. She won a game for every day I had been here. No money changed hands: there was already plenty at stake between us.

_____(GOING TO CRACOW)

The old red Mercedes hadn't been Wojciech's for long. He'd bought it off a student friend from Berlin who'd recently spent a week at his book-cramped Warsaw flat; it still had a German registration. Wojciech seemed a little uncomfortable with such a large car and, though I wasn't sure I could do any better in a Christmas fog which might last all the way to Cracow, I offered to drive.

"No, no," he said, remonstrating as if I'd insulted him. "Impossible."

"All right."

"Police maybe stop us, they see American passport, we are here one week. Unless you give money."

"All right."

There'd been no fog on leaving Warsaw, only flat fields with nothing moving and a fine white mist in between the birches and pines at the fields' borders. Occasionally the flatness was interrupted by the stone houses of a village. Sometimes the road ran near train tracks, but we saw no trains, and few other cars. Petrol was particularly scarce at this time of year. Maja had told me we wouldn't reach Cracow without the black market; one month's government ration of fuel wouldn't get us even halfway there.

Intricate cat's cradles of black telephone wires hung above the road, in this country where few telephones worked. In snowy fields, snowier as we crawled south, stood crosses wearing black overcoats, as if to frighten off non-Christians and crows alike.

After an hour we came into fog, and the fields and trees disappeared. At first we joked and remarked that the fog would end soon, but it didn't. A billowy whiteness wrapped us in and turned the road into a blinding wet cavern.

"I think," said Wojciech, choosing his words carefully, "there are no more important poets in West. What you think?"

"Perhaps you don't get many translations here," I said.

In his stifling Warsaw flat Wojciech had pulled Maja and me into the bathroom and proudly swept aside a curtain. Behind it was a bookshelf of forbidden mimeographed and stapled books, equal parts literature, rubbish, and political theory.

"Little bit translations," Wojciech admitted. "Is only my feeling. My instinct, you know. Important poems must come from East now. Poland. Czechoslovak. Hungary, maybe."

"The Soviet Union?"

He said, "Who is interested what Russian think? Russian never stop talking of boring Russian story, everybody know already. And all Russian poets like prostitute, in bed with government."

For Wojciech there was only one important living poet.

I wondered what Maja had told him about us. Perhaps she'd said plenty, and he was simply being discreet, keeping the conversation on himself. It was difficult to see conspiracy in that boyish face.

I said, "Did you ever visit Maja in Amsterdam?"

He looked at me as if I was joking. "She never ask. I will go, but she never ask. I don't care. Anyway, she is different now."

"Different how?"

"Not crazy like before. Not *free*. And she is old now." He was just warming up. "Still beautiful, eh? But old."

"Thirty-three isn't old. How old are you?"

"Twenty-nine. But *she* is old." He slammed the dashboard. "Like German car, heh-heh. Old because—" He said something under his breath in Polish. "Please. Window."

I stuck my head out of the window and felt the fog part around my forehead: it was like putting your face into a ghost. Gaunt shapes were looming on either side. A couple of car horns tooted feebly ahead of us, like distant tugboats.

"A bridge," I said.

"Bridge?" He frowned. "Too many kilometers to Cracow."

I said, "So why do you say she's old?"

"Too many kilometers!" He laughed. "You, me, many." He ran off several masculine Polish names.

"Rzupinski?" I said. At least he was a great musician.

"Trumpet?"

"Saxophone."

"Ah." He smiled. "Maybe she play saxophone with him."

I said, "Many lovers doesn't make someone old. I've had plenty of girlfriends. So have you, I'm sure. That's only experience."

He said, "Different for woman. Like car with too many drivers. But this one is like car who drive herself, no?"

I thought: Next we'll be discussing how smooth her gears are.

He said, "She is old because she have no future."

"No future? Come on."

"Is because everything is behind her on road. You see? What is ahead?"

"A Dutch passport, to start with."

Or me.

I didn't meet Benjamin until midsummer, a good month after Maja visited me for the second time in New York. I used several gigs with a guitarist friend in London as an excuse to cross the North Sea by ferry and visit Amsterdam for a week. Already I was toying with the idea of subletting my apartment for a season.

On a sunny morning in late July the ferry dropped me at the Hook of Holland where Maja and Benjamin stood outside the customs terminal in a breeze, waiting for me like a real family. Benjamin was pointing to some boats, his face turned away, Maja was in the broad straw hat she'd worn one afternoon in Port Stilton. Without a tan she was less glowing but I could see her features more clearly.

Now the boy noticed his mother had begun to walk toward me—I liked that she never hurried at this moment of greeting after long separation. Benjamin forgot the boats momentarily, and stared with a question all over his rapt face, no doubt comparing me as I was comparing him to photos we'd each seen, wondering if we'd ever meet.

Shimmering windows. The perpetual Dutch tidiness, seen from the train: flowers, modest brick houses like a child's well-assembled replica of a country; Maja's knowing hand insinuating itself between us on the seats; a fold-down table with a trembling paper cup of orange juice and a cheese sandwich. Facing us, Benjamin ate seriously and observed me surreptitiously and mostly looked out the window, where there was a world he was sure of. He hadn't asked to see my clarinet but he'd kept an unwavering eye on its transfer, following my suitcase, up to the baggage rack.

"You liked the little voyage across?" Maja said.

"I always enjoy boats." It was hard to keep my hands off her, even in this polite train of people reading their newspapers.

"Benjamin and I took the same boat to London two years ago. We had easy weather going across, but coming back there was a gigantic storm. Waves like big monsters. Very frightening. Nearly everyone was sick except Benjamin." She smiled expectantly at him.

This was a Maja I hadn't seen.

Benjamin eyed the stranger who spoke English and obviously had a secret understanding with his mother and yet was not Simon. He hadn't said a word to me. I wondered how good his English really was—Simon had insisted on speaking it to the boy, Maja had told me.

I said, as if to her alone, "He's lucky. It's a great talent, not to get seasick. I have a friend who gets seasick in a bathtub."

Benjamin said to me in a piping voice, "Do you know how many light-years it is to Alpha Centauri?"

"Let me think about that one. I don't think I do know."

"I know," he said with assurance. "Four years and four months."

"You sound like you know a lot about astronomy."

"I'm *fascinated*." His accent was softly English, with a kind of hum behind it. "The problem is that my reading isn't good enough in English. I can only understand their astronomy books for children. But I understand it in Dutch, in grown-up books."

This was my cue, so I said, "In that case you'll probably know everything already in the book I brought you."

Maja had alerted me about his overriding concern with nebulae and black holes and space adventures. His face lit up as I rummaged in my bag for his present, a thick astronomy encyclopedia complete with foldout star maps for both hemispheres and 3–D pictures of interstellar space. I had another gift for him, stashed away for later: a topographical moon map in plastic that faithfully reproduced every crater and peak. It'd been difficult, in a shop on lower Broadway that catered to astronomy and science fiction buffs, not to run wild on behalf of this boy I'd never met. I enjoyed a kind of retrospective envy—when I was Benjamin's age outer space was mainly odd paperbacks, a weak telescope, and a few clunky TV shows.

He took the astronomy encyclopedia from me very solemnly and rattled off a burst of Polish to Maja, who answered him firmly. He nodded to her, looked at me, took a breath, and said, "Thank you so very much for the thoughtful book."

He didn't look up from it for the rest of the journey, except when a star map needed refolding. He must've wondered what we were saying for that hour, our voices kept deliberately low. Or did he remember having seen this before, could he guess what it meant?

_____ (WARSAW)

One morning I was practicing in the back room when I heard the apartment door shut heavily and the elevator trundle up, pause, and descend. A few minutes later I went to ask Maja something and found only Lena. Maja had gone out, she said. "To meet her father for lunch, wasn't it?"

"That's right." I tried not to act surprised.

In Poland it always seemed that something was being kept from me, a secret withheld, and it always felt like bad news. I thought: This is simply a manner they have grown into naturally, it comes from forever having to give reports of petrol shortages, or currency devaluations, or austerity measures, or power blackouts, or a threatened resumption of martial law. No one ever walks in and says: By the way, free enterprise was just declared compulsory as of Monday morning, champagne and caviar all around.

I made tea and said, in my halting French, that I was

going out too, even on such a cold morning, but I needed her help first.

Together we pored over a city map and examined the notepaper with my elderly cousin's handwriting, while I tried to explain why I must find the man living at that address. I garbled the story but Lena gleaned that I wanted to try even without Maja to accompany me. Eventually we found the street, all the way across the city map, in an undesirable area of Soviet-built apartment buildings, row on row.

"Like huge inhabited gravestones," she said.

She could tell me where to catch the correct bus, and indicate on the map where to get off and walk. I'd have to fend for myself in locating which building in which block in which section.

"Near the end of the war," said Lena, "Hitler said he'd turned Warsaw into a place that no longer existed, only a name. You'll see, such areas have been the result. Someone should punish the architects."

It was bitter cold outside, and Christmas only two days away—here they celebrated on the twenty-fourth. We were invited to Christmas Eve dinner at the flat of Maja's mother and stepfather, whom I hadn't met yet. Benjamin was still staying with them, getting contentedly spoiled rotten.

Not far from Lena's building loomed one of the pathetic tourist hotels run by the government. They were all called Forum; this one resembled an artist's conception of 1999 from about 1958. Their run-down bars, terribly expensive by Polish standards, were considered interesting by some locals because they were an easy place to mingle with foreigners. As a result they were the worst places for any clandestine meeting, with everyone presumably watching everyone else. According to Maja the rooms were routinely bugged but the microphones, like the faucets, were mostly broken. This hotel's lobby had an exhausted and exasperated air, as if all the journalists and spies had gone home and only the Kowalskis from Chicago, in search of family roots and good buys on Russian beluga, had come to take their place.

I went in to look for a day-old *Herald Tribune*—Lena's shortwave was broken and I was famished for news. Past the lizard-tongued moneychangers sidling around the entrance, past the police spy pretending to be a moneychanger lurking just inside. Past the phalanx of ravishing blond prostitutes, so expensively dressed there could be no doubts what they were, so gorgeous that in the West they'd be fashion models or on the covetous arms of wealthy men. How tempting they looked, these tall sirens, after another dissatisfied night with Maja.

The foreign newspapers hadn't come in for days. That meant there was news of Poland in them, so they were banned.

After the morning's respite, it began to snow again.

In my frustrated state, walking through dreamy flakes to the bus stop, I saw glowing, unreachable goddesses everywhere, in the flickering glances that unerringly took me in as a foreigner, assessed me coolly, lingered an instant, and passed on. The snow exaggerated their vibrant beauty, their quick walk, their easy and natural swing which, unlike Maja's, held no hint of sex. It was an innocent flirtation abetted by scarves pulled up across their cheekbones—all those sweaters and layers you had to go through to get at them—but a flirtation no less direct, and almost emboldened. To speak with a foreigner would've been as daring an act, for many of them, as sleeping with a Polish stranger.

At least, in my exasperation, I saw it so.

Following Lena's instructions, I got on one of the buses with an accordion joint at its waist, like a segmented caterpillar. I stood in a herd of schoolgirls—gawky, long-limbed, chattering nervously, then falling silent. Maja had been one of them fifteen, twenty years ago: she'd have been tall and confident for her age, like that auburn-haired athletic one, the natural leader of a group.

The unheated bus was forever stopping to engorge ever more passengers. On the streets it was snowing like crazy, and my feet were stiff and dying in my new leather boots, bought the day before. I thought: I'll probably get lost, and spend the afternoon trying to find the address, then learn Dilko left yesterday for the country.

Lena had tried at first to convince me to take a taxi, or wait for Maja and go another day. But since Maja was too busy to help me find someone in her own confusing city, then to hell with her, I'd do it myself.

I had an address that had been good until about seven years earlier, and theoretically Poles didn't change residence very often. It'd come from Jeremy, an elderly cousin in New York on my mother's side and an ardent music lover—every few months I'd stop by for a good home-cooked meal while he played some rare rehearsal tape of Toscanini at full blast and his wife yelled at him to turn it down, stop frightening the traffic.

On learning I'd be in Warsaw, Jeremy had come up with the address of a musical colleague of my Polish grandfather. They'd even emigrated to England together, but this other man had made the solid career my grandfather hadn't, as a prolific ballet composer and music teacher in London. Years later cousin Jeremy, on hearing an obscure recording, had realized this composer had been my late grandfather's classmate at the conservatory, and friend afterwards in their adopted country; and Jeremy had tracked the gentleman down.

This story reached me after it was too late for my oc-

casional London visits—after the composer, who'd simpli-
fied his name to Dilko decades past, had moved back to
Warsaw. By now he would be an extremely old man, if he
was still alive. My cousin Jeremy had heard nothing for
years, since a last postcard in the late seventies which spoke
vaguely of illness. Probably Dilko was dead by now. But I
wasn't going to leave Warsaw without trying to find him.

Of course I'd assumed Maja would come along on my
search. She'd heard the whole story from Jeremy firsthand
in New York, and offered to help. She'd said herself it
would be easiest before Christmas set in, life stopped for
the holidays, and taxis became even scarcer. Along with a
visit to Cracow I felt this my great quest in Poland. She
knew its importance to me, and what had been her contri-
bution? A few days ago she'd confirmed that Dilko had no
telephone, didn't even exist, according to Information. I
could've learned that much myself—the operators all spoke
English.

And what were her reasons for tormenting me every
night on that rough floor-mattress, her naked back turned
toward me? I would lie awake for hours, aroused, trying to
persuade myself that our standoff was a result of her returning to Poland (deny it as she might), and thus would
pass. I saw we were both displaced people now; three
months earlier when I'd visited Maja in Amsterdam for a
week, nothing had been amiss in our lovemaking there. I
chose to believe that these heavy-blanketed Warsaw nights
of sharing a bed made enormous and unnatural by our lack
of intimacy would not last long, no longer than Poland
anyway.

It was perpetual afternoon in this city. I descended from
the bus and got snapped up by a biting wind, with great
white wraiths of an apartment complex hovering around
me. Not a person moved on the open boulevards between

these Soviet acts of charity, designed to dwarf any human spirit. None had any outside numbers. I ducked into one monster and was assailed by a stench of shit, garbage, and filthy water—Lena's building was a good sixty years older and still didn't have the intestinal problems of this one. The timer light didn't work, so I held the door open until I found the number of the building on a small metal plaque. This would take days, if I had to stumble around blindly in every unlit doorway.

And yet it seemed right to diligently search this frozen country for anything I could find of my grandfather. Over the years I'd thought on him repeatedly. I had precious little of his music, only a few folk-song settings for voice and piano that showed an unusual, almost bizarre harmonic sense and a keen instinct for how much a melody could accept. My mother and my two aunts claimed that a trunk of music manuscripts had been lost when he moved house in London, but sometimes the story was it'd been lost en route from Poland.

With a family to support, he'd been forced to find another profession—he was refused a license to teach music in England because he hadn't studied enough Latin. I often wondered what all his piano pieces and chamber music sounded like. Surely there'd been a clarinet sonata among them? I didn't imagine he'd been a great composer, but he'd gone down my road ahead of me. And many times over the years when I thought I was getting nowhere, the shape of his life used to make me more determined not to give up, not to hand over my life to something else. At the very least to carry through what was in our blood.

Back outside I kept heading into a wind that hurtled down the wide streets as if on a straight two-thousand-mile trajectory across the icy steppes of Central Asia.

I must've walked several miles among those concrete behemoths, trying to find some pattern in the arbitrary numbering. Occasionally people passed without even a nod, either propelled by the wind or launching themselves purposefully into its face. Behind the swaying buildings stretched an immense depth of gray sky, tier upon tier of clouds. Once in a while taxis rolled past, dinky Polish versions of Fiats or puttering snails from "Demokratik" Germany, always full of passengers squashed together as the little cars conserved petrol and fought the wind.

Two old ladies only shook their heads when I showed them the address, not even willing to look at it, and a shuddering young man in a thin jacket said, in a clearly enunciated, mocking English, "Better try them all!"

I was about to give up this fool's mission when, purely by luck, I found Dilko's building, clearly marked on the inside door. The timer light even worked. Ten stories: stairs, no elevator. The narrow hallways were each lit by an emergency bulb, dim and buzzing with alarm, and stank of recent human residue.

Jeremy had noted the apartment number for me. On the fifth floor I wondered if I'd gone too far; I'd counted thirty apartments on each floor, but few doors had numbers or names, and I couldn't figure out the system. There wasn't the war zone tension of apartment corridors in New York—it seemed a deserted prison instead.

I did some calculations, estimated that Dilko's apartment could be one of two at the end. I knocked politely on a door for a couple of moments and got no reply. On the other door I banged more insistently.

I heard voices, whispers, an urgent argument sotto voce. I kept rapping, with polite pauses to give them a chance to open up while making it clear I knew they were there and I wouldn't go away.

Footsteps. A woman's voice said something in Polish.

I said, "Can you please help me? I'm looking for Dilko."

The door was loudly unlocked at last. She looked startled from sleep: hair tousled every which way, clothes rumpled, her dreams interrupted. She might've been forty, or even a hard-pressed thirty. I thought: This is how Maja would look, if she hadn't left.

I proffered the paper to her, indicated the building and apartment number. I did my best to seem gracious even though I felt sure she didn't understand a word I was saying.

She shook her head and waved her hand as if denying a salesman's pitch. "Not here."

So she did speak English. She looked very worried.

"Is this his apartment?"

"No, no." She made a sorrowful tutting noise.

"Do you understand what I want?"

"*Tak, tak, tak,*" she said. "You look this man."

"That's right. Thank you for helping me."

"I don't know this man."

"Is this the building? The address."

"Is address. But not here."

There was a look of entrapment in her eyes, so acute that I wondered if she thought I might be from the secret police in some elaborate plot. She shivered, though the corridor was sweltering.

I said, "How many years you are here?"—falling into her grammar, to relax her.

She swallowed and thought, and said, "Nine year." She corrected herself hastily. "Seven year."

Perhaps Dilko had died and she'd taken his apartment.

"Please, do you know who lived here before?"

"I don't know."

I said, "Does anyone here speak English?"

I sounded obsessional even to myself, but what if Dilko

lived at the other end of the corridor and she was afraid to tell me?

She said with a quick gesture of dismissal, "Good-bye now," shut the door loudly and bolted it twice.

I stood there on the knife edge of frustration, listening to water dripping somewhere. Abruptly I felt fed up, fed up with both the Polish sarcasm and the Polish lack of reply, fed up with their absurd theater of always trying to be the powerful one in every conversation, of never being able to relinquish or offer anything but more tea without a struggle. I understood they were in a hopeless situation, but didn't their attitude toward each other only make the situation more hopeless?

And of course I was the soft American, who didn't know what real struggle was.

Methodically—I would never come here again—I knocked on every door along the corridor. O sleeping neighbors, awake! O eavesdropping neighbors, come answer to a vanished comrade! A Polish son who returned from England to disappear in this forlorn corridor, this very prison, seven years or seven months or seven days ago.

No one answered, of course, though from behind door after door I heard the same whispers of alarm. Those walls were thin, they'd heard my conversation with their neighbor, they were right to be careful. Hadn't they been suspicious of her when she moved in? And all this time she'd been living next door!

I said very loudly, "Dilko, are you there? Dilko? I'm Jeremy's cousin, he wanted me to see how you were doing. Dilko? Dilko! It's me, I'm the grandson of your old friend—"

I heard anonymous footsteps, four flights down: they stopped, the front door clanged, and someone went out to brave the snow.

This was all Maja's fault. Not mine. Nor the fault of these people I'd terrified or at least disturbed. If she'd sacrificed an hour or two, we could've come by taxi, she could've spoken to that young woman in Polish, and we'd have settled the question of Dilko once and for all—that wasn't asking much. Or was the problem that by asking, I was giving her an opportunity to say no, and being Polish, what could she do but seize it, to show who was stronger?

These people are primitives, I thought.

I was so angry, so claustrophobic in that hot building, sweating even with my overcoat unbuttoned, that I hurled myself down four flights of ill-lit stairs and outside without steeling myself. Unprepared, I was nearly knocked sideways, buffeted by the icy wind. It was almost a hundred-degree drop in real temperature Fahrenheit, and for a moment I was like a drunken man, reeling through snow that was piling up, not sure where I was going.

Then I remembered. I was looking for a taxi.

The main road to Warsaw was six or seven long blocks away. By then the crisp air had awakened me and I was shivering. It was after two and already the day was settling down to its close. The light was weak, a disenchanted light in the steady snowfall. A few cars passed, and one empty taxi that enraged me as it rolled on through the muddy snow, taunting me until it dwindled. I saw no buses.

I must've walked for an hour, getting wetter and colder. What on earth was I doing here, I kept muttering to myself, what a long way I had come in a week. I could easily imagine my New York flat as it might've been on a day like this in late December, the windows frosted with condensation. My narrow kitchen with its paint-acned fridge. My old bathtub like a porcelain Moby-Dick with stubby legs. The inadequate heat. The small upright piano I'd used to compose on, rented for six dollars a month. My great grimacing plaster bust of Beethoven, so honestly kitsch it was almost art. My books, my three hundred records, my bedroom where Maja had seemed such a passionate, playful woman. Her photograph had rested on my piano these many months—in profile against a tropical sky, looking tender and thoughtful in a red-sashed straw hat. Queer to think that bright snapshot had sent me trudging along this muddy cold road.

Best of all, my flat had been silent as a glacier. Even amid the horn symphony of Manhattan, during the day the only noises that reached me on the second floor in the back were the resounding doors and shuffling footfalls of my neighbors, or the staccato cry of my monthly friend the exterminator. I could practice all afternoon or give lessons without hearing a cheep from the traffic a hundred feet away. Evenings the kitchen air shaft of the five-story walk-up was filled with the voices of my neighbors eating, arguing, washing dishes, but I rarely cared, since I usually went out to work soon after they came in. I knew no other musician who'd stumbled on such affordable peace.

Squelching my way along, getting colder and wetter as the snow squalled down relentlessly, it seemed unbelievable how much work I'd just turned my back on in New York—what seemed unpredictable there looked like sheer wealth in this weather. Whenever I was in town I'd had a regular duo gig with the pianist at a supper club down in Greenwich Village on two dead nights early in the week. I had a few steady students. On weekends I invariably got at least a double gig with someone's quartet or quintet, or with my own trio; sometimes this actually meant a club where people came to listen and drink rather than to eat and drown you out. Not to mention the cocktail parties and hotel bars and weddings that paid serious money, plus the odd chamber music recital.

Another year or two and I would've had a record out on one of the small jazz labels; I had few doubts that such a first step would necessarily lead to a second record and the rest. That thought made all the awful big band gigs, the occasional lucrative subs on horrific Broadway shows, seem bearable and more than just money. It meant something to be able to play well all day long and through the night. I could perform for hours on an energy that seemed to come out of the depths of the earth—it was only when I put my horn down that any difficulties rose to greet me.

But returning from New Zealand, suffused with Maja (a luminous snapshot of her in my clarinet case), on walking into my apartment after two days of air travel, the this-is-your-life moment, I'd felt I was being sucked back into an empty bottle. Was there really much in motion for me here? My bags in the hallway, I stared round at my mostly bare white walls and swallowed the thought of how little difference it made to be home. Who cared if my playing was stronger than it'd been this time last year, or a year before that? The problem was that it wasn't absolutely, explosively, unmistakably recognizable among the din of other players competing for listeners' attention; it wasn't a voice bursting with individuality yet. Until it was, nothing would happen: my life would be years of steady here-and-there gigs, maybe a spot in someone else's group a little higher up the food chain, or with luck a record that a few fellow clarinettists would notice, and nothing more. It was as if I could foresee all of it, and that shook me. If the telephone had rung, some promoter offering to send me anywhere that night for another three months, I'd have accepted on the spot; but what seemed most missing was the feeling I'd left back by that New Zealand lake.

A taxi slowed, not wanting to risk getting stuck, so I was forced to run alongside and shout. I yelled the name of

Lena's street, he looked disgusted, so I yelled *"Stare Miasto!"* which meant the Old Town. I was a tourist, I would pay in hard currency. He leaned over and the passenger door sawed open, and a moment later I was snatched out of the wind, getting whisked along at thirty miles an hour, the windshield wipers mewing away at the snow and a draft biting at my calves from a gap in the floor. He offered me a cigarette and, for once in my life, I wished I smoked.

For five American dollars he took me to the Old Square. By this time the day was waning and I was overjoyed to know where I was, to have gotten my circulation back, and to imagine that Maja might even be a little worried at my lateness. Let her wait, I thought, let her live in hope and die in despair. Across the noble faces of the houses a delicate light was passing, as broken clouds came to rest on the clay-pot roofs.

Outside a warmly lit old café a trio was playing "Summertime," just by the steps up to that world of cakes and coffees and a fire. They wore mittens with the tips of the paws cut off so they could play. A competent bassist, a good guitarist, and a struggling alto sax player who mangled the melody; nothing robs you of enthusiasm like hearing the easy made difficult. A cloth guitar case lay open with a few coins in it. Not many.

God help musicians in weather like this, I thought. When they finished, the few passersby who'd stopped to listen moved on into the café or across the square. The three musicians watched them go, sighing; there were no contributions until I stepped forward. If they were willing to stand around in the snow trying to play jazz, I figured they deserved at least enough for one hot meal each. It was all too easy to imagine myself freezing in their shoes.

My last night in New Zealand, my bags packed, my mind dry after a long bath, I went down reluctantly to the hotel restaurant. A Maori waitress showed me to a table with a RESERVED sign; I was the first to arrive. Trying to arrange in my mind what I wanted to say to Maja before the night was through, if I got a moment alone with her. I could feel my imminent departure in my throat. It struck me sharply that she and I would have no more time together; yet here I was, asking her to give up a secure and familiar life, no matter how ultimately wrong it might look to an outsider. No, I should not dream.

It was raining lightly, a pattering tune on the lake, when she walked in, always punctual. In a sand-colored shift like a Roman toga she looked vulnerable, having been caught by the first drops. This dress too had been made by her Warsaw friend.

"Did you see Simon?" she asked immediately.

"Not yet."

"He must be in the kitchen." She squeezed my hand very quickly and fiddled with a dangling earring. "I can't accept that at this time tomorrow you'll be gone. And I might not see you another time."

I rapidly started dreaming again.

"You'll see me. In New York. Or Amsterdam."

"Everyone talks of New York. And no one ever comes to A'dam."

I pulled out an address card for her; I'd already written my friend Albert's number on the back. "If you leave a message and don't hear from me, it means I'm on the road. This man always knows how to contact me."

"What if he is not there also?"

"He never goes anywhere. He's a composer."

She said, "We don't have a telephone in that little house. But I'll call you. When I organize my ticket back to A'dam. To see if I can stop for a day or two."

She astonished me—she looked as if she might cry.

"You must excuse me," she said. "I'll be remembering you at this table next week. You'll be gone and I'll still be in this place by myself with nothing to do. Except find the courage to leave."

"That's a lot to do," I said. "Don't get stuck here. Leave, and don't come back."

"And if I do?" She smiled. "It's too far for a monkey to visit twice."

"So that's what you've decided? You'll return, to marry him?"

"I decided—you must surely understand already what I decided, no? I just don't act on the decision yet."

"That's backwards," I said. "You haven't really decided until you act."

I was imagining Maja's visit to New York: our stilted first conversation in the airport taxi, her listening to me play in a club that night. A few days of revealing the city to her. A couple of nights of Maja unfolding herself to me. Then her departure, several long-distance calls, and finally, perhaps, my turning up in Amsterdam. A venerable café, a waiter's starched face.

Just then Simon appeared. Upstairs I'd thought it might be possible to carry off the meal with aplomb, a man of the world, but now I felt sick at the prospect of an hour of slow Maori service.

He greeted me with a handshake of slightly dubious fellowship. He was taller than I remembered.

"How'd you get on with our lovely Maori g-girls?"

"Not as well as I'd hoped."

"I had the gist that Temani rather fancied you. Pity, she's off tonight."

"I missed some signals, then. Next time."

He said without irony, "It's hard to g-get very far in a couple of days. G-Guess they're not susceptible to your big city methods, eh?"

"I guess not. But it's wonderful how they're so at ease with themselves."

"They're like tropical birds. Forget what they're doing. Fly off halfway through the day. Not unlike certain other women I could name. Still, they're so friendly no one minds if the c-coffee arrives a little late."

His stammer was going like a firecracker. I wondered if he stammered as much when he wasn't with Maja. It seemed insidious, how he got away with crackling broadsides at her under the alibi of a speech defect.

She said to Simon, "He was telling me I should stop a few days to visit the States when I fly back. Perhaps New York this time."

Simon stared at me, a kind of surprised anger in his blue eyes—a club owner dismayed at the cost of good music.

I said to Maja calmly, "When would you come through?"

"That's anyone's g-g-guess," said Simon. "She always talks about leaving but—" He stalled, readjusted what he wanted to say. "Plays it loose. No action, mate."

"Wait a minute," said Maja. "You know I must be back in A'dam the first of April. To inscribe Benjamin for his school again in September."

"Good precaution," said Simon. "If he doesn't come out here."

He spoke as if genuinely convinced the boy would end up in New Zealand, not Holland. No matter how he treated Maja now.

"You know what they say about the school problems here," said Maja. "And what's there for him to do? This means he gives up all his holidays with my mother in Poland."

"Our little school isn't so bad." Simon turned to me, his fellow man, for support. "Fantastic g-growing up by a lake, eh? So he doesn't have the city in his veins all his life. The Maori g-g-girls will be downright crazy about him. Family-minded people."

I was ready to tell him what I thought of his family-mindedness, but the point was, after all, to convince her to leave the situation, not argue with the bastard myself.

"But he can't have a New Zealand passport, can he," said Maja. "Not for two years. And I'll lose my chance at a Dutch one."

As well as a flat and a job and a European life, I thought. But surely the boy would eventually get a local passport once she and Simon married? I felt at sea in this confusing world of refugee citizenships, passport regulations, semi-exiles, flexible frontiers; I could only ever be an amateur emigrant.

"Little domestic road repairs," said Simon to me. He took her hand affectionately. "I've had a puncture. You Yanks'd say I've g-gone flat."

He was putting on a bold front of her son being welcome out here, for my benefit, I supposed. He must've suspected that Maja had explained everything.

She said, "Tell me about New York."

"Just like in the shoot-'em-up movies," said Simon. "War in the streets. Tourists welcome till they get in the bloody line of fire. Right? Or am I putting too much sugar on it?"

"Lots of Polacks, no?" said Maja. "In Green Witch Village, I heard."

"All over, but you don't often see them as a group," I said. "They're not protesting or rioting or anything. Sometimes they march in parades."

"She doesn't like parades," said Simon. "Thinks they're always Marxist-Leninist."

"You two don't know what a real parade is," said Maja. "A real parade means they crush you whenever they want."

I told myself that to someone escaped from Poland, Simon must seem a handsome, stalwart soldier of the British Empire and a good potential father for the boy. I can't remember what else he and I talked about; perhaps hotels I'd stayed in on tour, since hotels were a thing we had in common. At some point he decided I was harmless—I was describing how much time I spent on the road, a scattered life, etcetera, obviously only a momentary threat to his hold on Maja. Satisfied, he could go back to work.

"Off to the mines." He stood up and we shook hands. He smiled wanly. "Drop us a card from the other side of the world, let us know if it's still there. Or if a bomb drops. We'll likely be here."

Maja waited until he was out of earshot before she said, "He and I always try to play a kind of chess with each other now. I'm so tired of all our strategies."

She seemed so on edge I thought she would end the evening then and wish me good night. I knew that that weekend in my apartment I'd think back on her facing me on the other side of the world, her hair about her cheekbones, and wonder what I was left with.

"I write this for you." She fumbled in her pocket for a slip of paper. "That's the post address here at the hotel. I write also the address of my girlfriend in Amsterdam."

Her English was breaking down.

"She will always know where to contact me, because she gets my money for me every month from the government."

"What money's that?"

"For Benjamin and me. The Dutches give money if you're an unmarried mother. Not much, about three hundred dollars. And next year they'll find us a better flat at a small rent. I'm on a list."

There was little real independence here, only the hunger.

"You're lucky to live in such a kindhearted country."

"I wish it was not this way, but—" She shrugged. "You must take a useful gift when it's offered to you, no?"

I'd been futilely waiting for the bill. One of the Maori waitresses finally loped over and waved her hand as if saying good-bye. She singsonged, "Oh, Simon said it was okay."

The phrase would reassure me for months.

"Can't we go for a walk along the beach?" I asked. "Or will that be too obvious?"

"It's all right," said Maja. "Not for long, though."

I still trust my memory of that conversation. What I can't swear by is my precise, slow-motion memory of the rest, after strolling by the lake beyond the hotel. A few drifting voices, a snatch of music, a backfiring car. As if by accident we found ourselves wandering toward the stretch of beach where we met. Skirting the water's edge, both of us barefoot. Maja's sandals swinging from her hand at my side. Past the chairs where we first sat. Hotel lamps winking through trees.

We entered the shadows and sat on the sand, where the beach was dry beneath overhanging branches.

It's from this evening on that I considered us lovers; at least we would no longer be only friends. In her letters she wrote as much to me: that evening would acquire a kind of power, would become what we steadfastly clung to until we saw each other again. Even though so little happened that night, later in New York when she collapsed into my arms and my bed it seemed a continuation of that walk by the lake.

With enough of a mist falling to keep everyone else safely inside, we had the beach all to ourselves. Crosslegged on the sand, facing each other, the lights from my hotel muted through trees behind her. A slender silhouette, weirdly reminiscent of a many-armed Hindu goddess of lust and death, her arms bare in her short toga-shift. I could almost hear her flesh sending me messages.

I leaned over and kissed her slowly, a long and exhausting kiss: for once there was nothing reluctant on her part. After a moment she drew away, and I gently tried to coax her backwards to the sand, but she refused by shaking her head.

She murmured, "I think this is where I want to start dreaming about you. Until I see you again."

No matter what she said, in the half dark she looked like one of those available Madonnas by Edvard Munch.

I said, "You remind me of a student of mine in New

York. She always practices only parts of pieces. Promising to put the whole work together for the next lesson."

My veiled plea wasn't lost on Maja. She said in measured tones, "Making love doesn't last very long," she said. "Five minutes? An hour? I don't care. Not even five hours. It's afterwards that I care. Do you believe we could ever make love and you go off and forget me? This doesn't interest me at all, because I know I won't forget you. But if this is all you want, I'll do anything you ask right now and you'll never hear from me again. But if—" She reached over and stopped my grunt of protest with a finger pressed firmly to my lips. "If you want to tease me by letter and know that I will also drive you crazy through the post, so that every other woman seems like a phantom, so that you are always wondering, all day long, when we finally see each other if you will hypnotize me like back in Port Stilton—" She withdrew her finger from my lips. "*This* interests me."

Then abruptly she was up and standing before me, a silhouette ten feet tall, shaking down her dress as she spoke. "We must go now. We can take a coffee at the hotel if you want. In front of everyone. You can tell me more about New York."

"So long as it won't cause you trouble."

"You have already caused much trouble. And you're going to decide I'm not someone loyal, because I'm doing this behind Simon's back. I was not looking around for such a situation, you know. I didn't start imagining until you kissed me after the dance."

She reached out her hands and pulled me to my feet.

"It's your decision, too," I said.

"Do you think anyone decides?" she asked quietly. "It's there immediately between people, no? And then they go forward or perhaps they hold back."

"That first morning when you told me you had a boy-friend here, I couldn't believe it."

"I don't see why. I'm not so bad, you know."

"It didn't seem possible that—that someone would put salt on the pastry."

She said with amusement, "You make me sound like something you get fresh every day for a few pennies. At any shop around the corner."

I started to protest until I realized she was joking.

She said, "But perhaps the salt is what makes the pastry more interesting. This is what Dante wrote about exile. 'Other men's bread is salty, other men's stairs are steep.' You don't know the difficulties, how it feels living in another man's country." She touched my cheek very lightly. "And it may be that in another way, for you other men's pastry will always taste more delicious. Did you never think this may be why you're with me?"

I didn't say anything.

"Anyway, perhaps I'll get sweeter. Or saltier and saltier. It depends on what we write to each other."

So I was with her. I knew at that moment that this was what I wanted to hear her say. Now I could leave.

_____ (W A R S A W)

After the failed mission to find my grand-father's friend Dilko, it was well into eve-ning when I reached Lena's flat and found a party in progress.

All the sofas and throw pillows and armchairs were taken. Wojciech was there, and Andrzej and his wife; plain Magda was slicing mushrooms as I entered and smiled at me apol-ogetically; Zosia looked like an elegant gypsy, her black hair done up in a bun held by an elaborate antique pin. Ulrik, enormous in a corner chair, poured shots from a vodka bottle which he kept on a table within easy reach. Everyone was talking at once and music playing, Poland vs. the An-drews Sisters.

There were others I hadn't met, including a handsome couple who must've been in their late forties. The woman had fading blond hair, dressed casually, and was still se-renely beautiful, with an actress's care in her gestures, and a vulnerability I rarely saw in the faces of Polish women. The man wore jeans and a thick sweater; beneath wavy gray hair a vein bulged in his high forehead. An almost aristocratic face. With one hand holding a leg crossed over, he listened attentively to Lena, who was making her point earnestly. All the while, he cased the others in the room, scanned me, moved on.

Despite my grumbling during the day, I felt almost at home in this flat, welcomed back to the endless conversation of these impromptu Warsaw gatherings—people never gathered so regularly and informally in New York. Poles seemed proud of the unhappiness and impossibility of their position, proud that they could be happy in a situation which would make nearly anyone else bonkers.

Maja glided over—relieved, I was gratified to see, that I'd arrived at last. She was wearing makeup, a rare occurrence: I rapidly deduced her decor must be for the benefit of the man speaking with Lena.

Maja said, "What's all that you're carrying?"

"Orchestral scores. I found a music shop."

It'd been a few blocks from the Old Square, in a rebuilt eighteenth-century house—windowed cabinets, prim shopgirls, and a severe matron in charge. A good deal of giggling and bustling at the foreigner's presence. Half the music had evidently lain there for decades, regularly dusted in meticulous piles, and none of it had been printed in the West. I'd asked for Penderecki, Poland's greatest living composer, but they carried none of his scores. I had all their clarinet music already, except for a set of technical studies written in the fifties by a Hungarian I'd never heard of. I bought the book out of a sense of duty and watched two shopgirls wrap it in brown paper.

The price was about fifteen cents. I questioned it twice and realized that, as with my boots, I was operating on a black market exchange rate, and everything here was already ridiculously cheap by Western standards anyway. I asked the matron for permission to go behind the counter to one glassed-in cabinet that held several shelves of pocket orchestral scores. They can run fifteen dollars or more in the West; these, printed in Leipzig or Budapest, Prague or Cracow, cost pennies. I scooped up new editions of Prokofiev and Debussy and Haydn and everyone else; it was easier to buy than to choose, they were so cheap. At first the shopgirls were astonished, then they started wrapping with a vengeance—it was hard convincing them to wrap the scores in three packages, not individually.

Now I opened one package to show Maja what I meant. She glanced in, like a cat sniffing at a foreign substance, and said, "They must've been surprised at the American buying the entire store."

"Only at first. They were pleased, like shopkeepers anywhere."

She said, "You don't think it's insulting, for a foreigner to come in and buy as if the local money doesn't mean anything?"

"Don't be ridiculous. They were all smiles. I'd like to go back another day."

She said, "Well, there's nothing to stop you. You seem to be able to find your way around by yourself."

"It's not so difficult, when a beautiful woman takes the time to draw you a map." That stopped her. "Lena," I added. "The only person around this morning."

Maja made a mock-bored face. "Why are you Americans so sentimental? By the way, we have to stay awake. The French are arriving tonight. Lena's friends. Their train is a day late."

Her tone and her whole attitude irritated me, but this wasn't the moment to start an argument.

"And who are all these people?"

She said, as if it weren't obvious, "Polish people. There might be someone here no one knows, it's impossible to tell. Look, Ulrik is very drunk, so if he proposes some fantastic plan to you, just say we'll do it."

"Do we have to listen to the Andrews Sisters all the time?"

"Don't you like them? Oh, there's great news. A New Year's Eve party we are all invited to. *Very* exclusive. About five thousand *zlotys* a ticket. We dress up—what do you call it? Like a carnival."

"A costume ball. Who are those two?"

She said, "Josef is a playwright. A very good one. His wife was a film star here. Teresa. And a theater actress. She stopped doing films a few years ago. She's still beautiful, no? I think she does only theater in his plays now. I knew them many years ago but not very well. They were important already and I was still only in university. I suppose he must speak English. He's always going to the West to give lectures."

Andrzej came over and shook my hand rather formally, his arm around my shoulder and his breath like a vodka tornado at my ear. He said, "First, martial law. Now, the fucking Andrews Sisters. This is what we've come to in my country, man. The end of the road. On second thought—" He cocked his ear at the music. "Maybe martial law wasn't so bad."

Maja left us to join the important people.

I said, "Andrzej, do you want to strike a blow against the Andrews Sisters? Do you want to hunt them down like helpless little animals in the snow?"

He peered at me. "What are you talking about? I mean that very seriously."

"Tell me about the rhythm section on Rzupinski's old recordings."

He blinked and scratched his ponytail as if it were a lucky rabbit's foot that helped him think. "Let me see, that was—" He ran off two unpronounceable names, paused, and added a third. "They got fed up with him. They played with a big band for a long time. With a chick singer. Not Wanda Warska. The other singer. Doesn't matter. She moved to Berlin to marry and have half-breed babies."

"But the rhythm section is still around?"

"They must be. I don't keep up with these people any-more, you know." He winked conspiratorially. "I'm like the government, I've got a ten-year plan of my own. They're investing in tractors, I'm investing in autobiography. One day—" He swept his hand around the unattainable vistas of Lena's flat; I could see him happily installing his clutter here, his lost art. "One day this will all be my wife's."

I said, "Could you get hold of those three musicians for me? I thought I might try to make a record while I'm here."

"A little East meets West, eh? They'll overcharge you."

"That doesn't matter. It happens in New York, too."

"That doesn't matter. Suppose they don't let you take the tapes out? That doesn't matter? Look what happened to me. You'll have to get Ulrik to smuggle them for you. He *is* a smuggler, by the way. You know why he doesn't get caught? Because he looks like a smuggler. So he appears to be faithfully fulfilling his role in the system. That's all any official really cares about."

"What does he smuggle?"

"Ask him yourself. What do I know? Slandering a friend. I'm a simple painter. He's certainly not smuggling—" Andrzej was blown sideways by gales of wheezing laughter; he was far drunker than I'd thought. He kept himself upright with one hand against the wall until his laughter subsided, and he recovered and said, "Excuse me. I mean, certainly not paintings. Not that gorilla. Look at him, man. Hey, Ulrik! Do you miss the jungle? Swinging through the trees?"

Ulrik waved stonily from his perch beside the vodka.

"What a shame," said Andrzej tenderly. "He would have made a great party official."

Someone turned on the television. The news was in progress and everyone shushed everyone else and piled around it. Wojciech even turned down the Andrews Sisters. Reagan came on the screen, a motionless photo smaller than the female announcer's head.

"I think," said Magda hesitantly to me in a whisper, "I know I am wrong, but I think he is still handsome."

Only Ulrik remained behind the television, nodding moodily at the announcer's clipped sentences and grimacing from time to time. He caught me watching him—I'd joined Maja, on the sofa arm. He said in a loud voice, "Your president says the Soviets are an evil empire, they must be exterminated like red Indians. Like rats." He shook his fist at the happy prospect of so much slaughter. "Finest president since Lincoln. Finest man who ever breathe."

"I hate Nancy Reagan," said Maja to me, then embarked on a diatribe against her in Polish that had people smiling but not laughing. I kept silent on the sofa arm and wondered what these people knew of Maja and me. Had she introduced me as her lover? Did she tell people we lived together in Amsterdam? Or that I'd come all this way just to experience Poland during the Christmas holidays?

She and Wojciech were sharing a joke, he squatting before her in that unnatural position which always has something of a lover's supplication. For all I knew she'd resumed her old affair with him during those afternoon visits with her father or mother that I was rarely invited on. Perhaps everybody in the room knew this but me, perhaps this was why she kept me at arm's length in that airless back room with the uncomfortable mattress and the unsold paintings of intergalactic lovers naked in the gyres of the cosmos. Probably I was simply imagining things: in a foreign country where everyone around you talks nonstop and you don't understand three words of the language, your mind runs quickly to desperate conclusions.

Tonight, I thought, no matter how much I've drunk, no matter how tired, I will not take no for an answer.

I got up and walked around Wojciech and Maja's conversation—I assumed he was talking about his poetry, because he looked so very resolute—and fetched myself another glass of red wine. When I returned the news had ended and a familiar theme, saccharine strings in a heavenly glissando, was pouring out of the television. It was *The Sound of Music* (that opening on the Swiss mountaintop), and once again people stopped talking to listen and watch.

Unbelievably, Maja said to me, "Beautiful film, don't you think? They show it every year at holiday time."

Magda and Zosia nodded agreement. A bony guy in spectacles settled himself closer to the TV. Ulrik raised a glass to the von Trapp family and the Andrews Sisters surrendered at last. How could these cynical people, deliberately surprised by nothing, find delight in this Broadway treacle?

Andrzej said to me softly, "When I was sixteen I used to dream that one day I would teach that woman a lesson." He meant Julie Andrews, but he was also looking at the playwright's lovely wife, Teresa, who was watching the film and perhaps thinking: Had I lived in Paris, or New York, or London . . .

I patted Andrzej on the shoulder and cut over to join Josef and Teresa, who'd remained at the long dining table. She was at the end near the television, he sat several chairs away. The crowd had stranded him, sipping wine, when the news came on.

I said, "Do you mind if I join you?"

"Not at all." His English was confident but heavily accented.

I indicated the rapt faces. "Did you ever write for the movies?"

"Not for such movies," he said. "When I was young, for some experimental films. They were a mess. This was 'sixty-eight. Are you old enough to remember 'sixty-eight?"

"Of course."

He chuckled. "I thought the European 'sixty-eight was not taken so seriously in the States. You had your own version, I think."

"That's right. But everyone noticed Prague."

"I was in Prague then," he said. "By accident. If you're a writer usually you look for such events. Here in Eastern Europe, if you stand in a doorway long enough, a catastrophe finds you and you have to decide if that's what you want to write about or not." He smiled. "I'm sorry, I was in London last week giving a lecture, I can't stop repeating myself. If I'm not careful I shall expect you to applaud when I finish talking."

I said, "I never realized it was so easy for Poles to travel. I always thought you couldn't leave Poland when you wanted."

"I suppose the government is satisfied that if I wanted to desert the ship I would have done so long ago. I criticize them in my work, but I try to write about other subjects also. A hundred years from now, how much political art will be interesting? Politics is turning us into bores—if the Soviet army ever leaves, no one in Poland will have anything left to talk about. We'll be reduced to watching American musicals."

The television was singing, the people around it chattering. Maja and Zosia were laughing at some great joke, the glow of the film on their faces in the lamp-lit room. I heard the words "New York" in their conversation, and Lena chimed in while the others listened attentively. For years I'd been ready to leave the city at a moment's notice, yet it still made me uncomfortable to know they were insulting it—Maja had put on her disparaging voice.

Reverse psychology at work, for no matter how Poles bicker and complain about our culture, the United States is still an antidote to all the propaganda they're forced to swallow. Once they arrive they swear they'll leave next week and never return, but as soon as they swan back to Warsaw with their grandiose stories they try their best to drive everyone crazy with jealousy.

Josef said, "And what do you do? For a profession?"

He was the first and last person in Poland who asked.

We talked for a few minutes about music; he had the writer's habit of asking questions that appear aimless but are in fact full of purpose.

I said, "Look, I don't understand something. You're a man of standing in the world, I'm sure you could move to Paris or Berlin or London and continue your career. Why on earth do you stay here?"

He said, "You don't like it here?"

"Everyone's so frustrated—people have to stand in line even to buy a bar of soap. And yet they're close enough to the rest of Europe to have an idea what they're missing. I don't see why someone like you would willingly come back."

I expected him to answer with aging parents and a flat they swore they'd never leave. Instead he said, "All that you notice is true. And what you see is only the peak of our iceberg. Teresa and I don't stay either for political reasons. I am not optimistic enough to believe there will be a change anytime soon."

"So why do you stay?"

He poured us both more wine before he spoke.

He said, "Why? It's not the Bulgarian wine, which you must be tired of. I always say, because of the strong feelings between people here. Every Pole prefers other nationalities to his own, but no matter where Poles move, they stay together. Like bees around their private hive. You try to put your hand in from outside and you get stung."

"Or perhaps you find the honey," I said.

"Perhaps. But what they miss when they leave is an intensity of relations. Here their friendships and enemies— arguments—seem more powerful than anywhere else. There is passion in every bond because it's against the scenery of this tedious and awful political situation. It's like we are people waiting for a war, and we don't know whether we want it or not. Because who can say what it might bring? So there's not much we can do except wait, and learn to live in the waiting more than people elsewhere live in the doing." He frowned. "Maybe I'm wrong. But whenever I was outside Poland, it seemed people's relations with each other were not so strong. They were like bottles with important labels but with not such a special wine inside."

"Do you have children?"

"Unfortunately, not." He tapped his glass nervously and I understood that it was not through lack of trying. "If we had, we would have left a long time ago. I would not force a child of mine to inherit this situation if I had the alternative."

"Doesn't it help here to be a writer, or an actor, or a painter? In the States if people haven't heard of you, they think you're a crank or a fraud. Here the arts seem to give you a certain prestige. Almost a glamour."

He said, "It's only the same respect people have for—how do you say? An endangered species. No one really admires the dodo bird, but they still stop talking to watch the last ones go by. Don't forget, it also helps here to be a party member."

Ulrik, on his way to the bathroom, said heavily, "This is the only party in Poland I want to be a member of. Right here."

Josef said, "Look, there is one thing you must understand about this place even if you take back nothing else. People in the rest of Europe, in the States especially, look all the way over to Eastern Europe. Maybe they know we are not all the same but they think we are all under the same gravity. The same pressure. That is not right, eh? This is the freest country in Eastern Europe. You mustn't ever forget that. And we have kept ourselves a little naive, too. This is why Poles almost never fake anything. We haven't learned how. One day, eventually, we will learn. Then—" He issued a barking laugh. "The world had better watch out."

I wondered if the strong red wine was hypnotizing us both, because our conversation seemed to be disconnecting, wavering, blurring before my eyes. I said to Josef, as if confiding a secret, "You know, the problem is that in the West, people tell each other Polish jokes. But no one knows who the Poles tell jokes about."

He said, a little puzzled, "Why, the Bulgars, of course. Despite this wine, they are the stupidest people anywhere. But not only the Bulgars. You want to hear a genuine Polish joke?"

"Absolutely."

Years from now, I thought, I'll dine out on the Polish joke told me by the great Warsaw playwright, Josef Someone, while the snow multiplied outside and the wine flowed inside.

He said, "There's an American man. In the States some-where. He's in love, desperately in love, with a beautiful Polish woman. So he goes to his doctor and explains the situation. The doctor says, Well, where's the problem?

"And the man answers, Doctor, the problem is that she says she'll only marry me if I become a Polish man. You've got to help me. What can I do?

"The doctor says, My friend, I can help you, but this is a very serious operation. To make you into a real Polish man we must take out one-half of your brain.

"The man says, If that's the only way, Doctor, let's go ahead.

"So the doctor gives the anaesthetic and performs the operation and is standing by the hospital bed as the man wakes up. When the man's eyes open the doctor says to him, Look, I don't want to worry you, but there's some good news and some bad news. The good news is that this extremely dangerous operation went very well, you're healthy and you're surely going to live a long time.

"The bad news is that I made a small mistake. These things happen, you know. By accident, instead of removing half your brain to make you a normal Polish man, well, unfortunately I took out three-quarters of your brain.

"The man raises himself up in bed, slaps his head, and cries, *Ai! Mama mia!*"

Teresa, at the end of the table, had a smile that would reach the back of any theater. She said to her husband in broken English, "Josef, I never will care even if half your brain is gone."

"I don't believe you," said Maja. "You find this com-poser's flat and they don't ask you in for tea?"

It was nearly midnight. The television film was long over, the von Trapp family had squeaked through to liberty, the guests were gone. We were washing up the plates and the wine and vodka glasses, Ulrik having murdered a bottle of Wyborova single-handed.

Lena had left a few minutes earlier, after a call from a friend at the train station to say that at last the Paris express would be arriving, seventeen hours late. A slight border delay, it seemed.

"Not *they*," I said to Maja. "It was just one woman. I don't know what it meant to her that I was looking for Dilko. Maybe he lived in her apartment before she did. Maybe he was asleep in the back room and she thought I was with the CIA, I don't know."

"You mustn't blame the CIA for everything."

"Your secret police, then. I don't know what she understood. She looked terrified. So she certainly didn't offer me tea."

"I never heard of a Polack who didn't ask a stranger in for tea," said Maja, her arms up to her elbows in suds. "You must have not been polite. Because she wouldn't be rude to you unless you were rude to her."

"I was as courteous as could be. It's a shame you couldn't come along, it was very frustrating. I'm not sure what to tell my cousin Jeremy. They corresponded for years."

She heard the reproach in my voice. She said, "Tell him how difficult it is to find someone here. You don't look them up in a directory and that's the end of it."

"I can see that."

Maja said, "Was she a young woman?"

"About your age."

"So you see, she thought perhaps you wanted to rape her. There's more crime here than you imagine. Not like Berlin or New York, but you probably frightened her. It would maybe seem a trick. You show her an address, and pretend you don't speak the language."

"Perhaps that's it."

I didn't want to hear her theories; she was only trying to obscure the fact that she hadn't been willing to accompany me, and that all my failure was her fault.

I said, "Next time I'll take along an interpreter."

"You could've had one this time. But you were determined to go today. You should have waited until after the New Year, when I will be more free. Then we can try again, if you like."

I said, "You said yourself the best time was before the holidays. You know how much it means to me to find him."

"Was she good-looking, the woman?"

"I couldn't tell. There wasn't much light in the corridor."

"Maybe right now she is thinking to herself that she wishes she asked you in. You never know, maybe you would still be there."

"I'd still be lost in the snow, trying to get a lift."

We heard the grunt and clank of the elevator, starting its difficult ascent.

"That will be Lena," said Maja quickly. "She told me these friends are having difficulties with their marriage. Probably they will be divorcing. So who knows what the situation will be like with them here." She dried her hands and ran her fingers quickly through her hair before a small square mirror propped above the sink. "Look, do you still imagine visiting Cracow?"

"Of course. My grandfather lived there for years."

"We can go for Christmas," she said. "We eat dinner the night before with Benjamin and my mother. Then we travel on Christmas Day. Because I think Wojciech is driving there, we can get a ride with him. Easier than the train."

The elevator was grinding upwards.

"So long as we stay somewhere on our own," I said.

"Why not? There are plenty of beautiful old hotels in Cracow."

"What's Wojciech going for?"

I was worried that he was, in fact, going only to accompany us.

"He has two sons there. A little older and a little younger than Benjamin. With a woman who is a big pop star here. A monster. It is over between them since a few years now. But Wojciech is still in love with her, no matter what I tell him."

I said, "There's no reason to be jealous of a monster, is there?"

For some reason I felt like aggressively upping the ante in our conversation.

The elevator wheezed and clattered to a halt ten feet away.

Maja said, almost with disappointment, "*I'm* not jealous. But if you were not with me here, Wojciech is ready to start our affair again."

And unbolted the door.

_____(N E W Y O R K)

Her first letter had reached me in Manhattan less than a week after I returned
from New Zealand—a weightless blue airmail puzzle whose
fragile flaps had to be gently unpeeled, detached, and un-
folded like a magician's crate, with more insides than out-
sides and handwritten messages on every surface. It stood
in my narrow mailbox downstairs, a traveler undaunted,
having made it all this way without being crushed or wrin-
kled. Its particular blue, a regal, ex-British, once-imperial
cobalt, looked exotic among the utility bills and performance art announcements.

It was snowing, an end-of-February wind rattling my
windows. I shivered, having gone down the single flight of
stairs in my bathrobe, for the mail came early and I got up
late. Would she have written me so promptly to tell me she
wasn't coming?

In fact she'd written the letter before I left Port Stilton.

Surprised, kochany? *I want you to imagine me on our beach, since this is where I am lying in the sun. Before our dinner with Simon. You are still here but I send this so you get something from me directly after you return. Perhaps I am imagining too much—that a young man in New York will have any reason even to think about someone thousands of kilometers away who feels trapped and frustrated with her life. I already miss you, I already regret that I didn't tell you clearly what it meant to hear you play for me. I lived with a great musician long enough to hear another one. But you know this already. Do I need to tell you how strongly this pulls me? Or perhaps you guess. Or perhaps you are not telling me the truth, and another woman is there looking past your shoulder as you read my words . . .*

That flushed moment of confirmation was like standing in a geyser of light: she wasn't wishful thinking or a mere encounter abroad, she was not a creature of my imagination. A couple of years ago I threw out a fat crinkly bundle of most of her letters. Now I wish I'd saved more of them—though perhaps, years on, like a perfume gone stale in a cupboard, they might've lost their magical scents and seem only tinted water.

Anyway, the letters arrived in their clockwork way, every Monday and Thursday, a pattern that followed particular flights from Auckland to JFK. Sometimes there were post-cards also, with an enigmatic suggestion scrawled in that handwriting which always reminded me of the tight knot on a balloon. Though we corresponded for little more than the month of March, it was like an extended summer to bask, even from afar, in the laser beam of her attention.

Her letters grew longer, often seven or eight pages, both sides, not those foldout contraptions. Sometimes it was local gossip, or telling me about Polish poets I'd never heard of,

or news of her son, whom she was anxious to see. Sometimes she quoted me poems:

Where are the others whose love was real and strong?
Should she remain faithful who didn't want to be faithful?

Most often she wrote me about how much she was looking forward to being in Europe again, and possible travels—
Brazil, Uruguay, Kenya—though she never explained how
or when or for how long. She made it clear she was on the
verge of leaving Simon, but the decision was a difficult one.
I would read and reread and practically memorize each
salvo with a growing sense that it was up to me to persuade
her, that we both knew what we were up to. And soon, in
an otherwise innocuous paragraph, for the first time she
told me she was in love with me.

To fall in love is to risk believing in yourself as only a
stranger can, no matter what you know. I wrote her at
equal length, trying to make my life sound fascinating rather
than hard scuffling work, trying to remind her how much
world there was out here, waiting. In my letters every gig
and street corner was full of eccentric characters, each with
his wisecracks and private obsessions; some I had to exag-
gerate. After five weeks of her letters our relationship by
mail far outweighed the little time we'd actually spent together.

Kochany! *(it means exactly = darling)*
You will think I am crazy, but I am still glad we didn't
make love here, no matter how much we want to now. I
remind to myself that we have all the time ahead of us we
want, to give what we like to each other. And I know because
we waited there will be nothing complicated in a bad way
between us when the moment arrives. You maybe don't ap-

*preciate how it is important to me that you still have kept
wanting me through this time.*

*So I am sending you a photo to make you want me a little
more. (Temani took it, on the far beach you never saw.) To
give you something to dream about. Next week I send you
my other side.*

*I hope you are also dreaming about . . . the tip of my
tongue. . . .*

Still, how long could our expectations be kept at a boil
with nothing definite arrived at?

Or perhaps this capacity to prolong the waiting is why I
put off making my own record for years. After all, six
months later I'd fail to leave New York when she urged me
to hurry and join her. Thus, she could argue, the conse-
quent erosion of her feeling was my fault; and I behaved
just as selfishly as she did, later, in Poland, which was where
these accusations took place.

I'd been back from New Zealand for a full month when
she telephoned. Long before I heard her speak I knew it
was she, from the tense crackle over the wire as if her per-
sonal voltage were being passed across the world, then the
click and gulp of the satellite bounce over the International
Date Line.

"Did you get my letter?" she asked, when the crackle
made way.

"You mean the important one?"

"It's more important to me than you think."

We had to speak at the top of our voices.

"When are you coming?"

"Next week. On the seventh. I stay a few days only, then
I go to Amsterdam. Because Benjamin is waiting. And his
school wants my signature for next year. So I buy the
ticket?"

"Absolutely."

She said, "I don't want to spend my money on the phone. I write you already with the plane information." There was a click suggesting a second minute and she added, "I hope you're saving plenty of energy for me."

"I am, it's been very cold here."

I heard her chuckle, the international connection died, and two weeks later she was wandering the apartment in my bathrobe, yawning after three planes and a shower. Barefoot, resplendent in her tan. When I followed her into my tiny darkened bedroom I found her lying on her side, limned by a single sheet, a long body in the shadows. My bathrobe bunched at the foot of the bed.

She said softly, "Can you shut the door? I want to pretend we're on a beach at night. Not New Zealand but somewhere else. Our beach."

I sometimes feel that it's not later, but when you first make love with someone new, that you're most yourself. Like playing a tune for the first time: you're nervous, uncertain, you're feeling your way, it's easy to get lost—but your response is still original and genuine simply because you don't know what you're supposed to sound like improvising on this new melody.

She'd propped her head on both pillows so she could watch me. My hands began, a little tentatively, to discover her through the sheet. Resisting the urge to hurry, to pull the sheet swiftly off her. I took my time tugging it from her bare shoulders but no further while running my hand almost accidentally up the draped length of her, feeling the tensile strength in her legs. Through the thin cotton I could kiss her breasts as if double-tonguing two stiff reeds, halves to quarters to eighths.

As I shifted onto the bed I felt her hands unbutton and undo me, pulling my trousers down. And then before I knew it she'd rolled across me and wrapped me in swirling bedclothes and she was naked atop the sheet, teasing me, torturing, floating.

"I've got you now," she murmured, biting at my ear.

With unnerving accuracy she settled on me, tormenting every which way. She began sliding the sheet down my chest—my hands roaming her back, her audacious curves— and at that long-awaited moment all my self-assurance, the glib facade of an amateur, fell away, for I went inexorably soft, soft, soft against her.

I'd felt this approaching, even though such a hasty retreat wasn't a frequent nervous tic of mine. As excited as I was by Maja, I sensed I was out of my depth. It was as if I'd been up there onstage, playing to my heart's content, then looked over at the other clarinettist and realized it was, say, Buddy de Franco—one of those masters who doesn't care what tune, he will explore every inch of it. The nature of any professional musician is to know clearly how good you are, and this carries over into the rest of your life. You learn all too soon when the most you can do is to try not to get blown off the stage.

Immediately I tried to pretend that my failure was strategy, not unease, even though I knew she knew. I pushed her off me and back onto the pillows, dove for her nether regions and began another approach, as if the issue wasn't my readiness but hers. She accepted this for several minutes—I was making moist headway but felt acutely the cool night air from the open window on my withered soul. My concern must've been legible to her, for she put her hands on my shoulders and gently pushed me back. A tongue of ornate gold-embroidered velvet and silk from the six-teenth-century Polish court of Christian poet-kings went to work on me, and ten seconds later I'd sprung back to life.

She was taking no risks this time. She clamped her legs

around and settled herself on me; in an instant I sank upwards and was gripped in a continuous accelerando of interior muscles that caressed and squeezed and tugged up,
around, and down. She wasn't out for her own ecstasy, or
even simply pleasure. She was trying to win me over to her
religion forever, kissing me ravenously, nipping at my
tongue, nibbling at my ears, flawlessly reading my slightest
signals below. I thought: This will be over in no time.

I couldn't move an inch without great effort. She would
let the fire die down very slightly, then stir the coals to a
blaze again. All I could do was circulate my hands as she
leaned back and away, still pinioning me.

The scant light from the other room caught like a vo-
yeur's flashlight her flat belly. I watched her navel revolve
as she began a kind of jangling Oriental dance with me
socketed inside her. I wouldn't have been surprised if
torches had flared in the night, cymbals begun to clash, and
cobra music started grinding away. Instead a low humming
began, a murmur that had strange chromatic glisses and
uneven rhythmic motifs and thick syllables packed densely
together. It was a few seconds, my imagination elsewhere,
before I realized Maja was singing softly to me in Polish.

I couldn't move, I didn't need to move. All I had to do
was stay firmly afloat, like a log raft in a storm-tossed sea.
Here was a Maja as responsive and willful and passionate
as I'd hoped. It was bliss finally to be joined to her; bliss to
pull my hands back down her sweat-sheened flanks, cup-
ping her bottom like pulpy exotic fruit, humid with exer-
tion; bliss to try to taunt her, to nudge her spine upwards
ever so slightly and provoke a bitten-off caw in her hummed
song; bliss to find my own axis at last and pivot against her,
so that she could only give in or accelerate. Bliss to feel her
indecision, to achieve a few instants when she was not in
control.

But I had to admit defeat, and sooner or later surrender: no man could've lasted long against her sophisticated onslaught. Barbaric doom appeared from nowhere and everywhere, like a massive volcanic eruption of orchestral sound that takes even the conductor by surprise in its poured fury and lava intensity. Maja felt it coming before I did, her seismograph more accurate than mine. As if utterly of her own volition, as if she could've chosen her own moment whenever she wanted, Maja agreed to coincide with my explosion, and bucked and writhed silently, gripped my thighs with her own and held me shaking against her as I let out a war whoop and slowly expired. She didn't make a sound, but I did have the satisfaction of seeing her arms straining, outstretched behind her head, fingers splayed in the pillows, as she came and came.

(I was drained dry. Already returning to myself, collapsed away from her, with that strange sensation of having lost a limb.)

Carefully she wriggled free of me and I drooped out. I wondered if I'd still know how to walk.

"You were wonderful," I said quietly.

She opened her eyes. "You're sure?"

She shook her head to fling sweat from her hair and flexed her arms in a kind of exultation and said, "You make too much noise."

"You made me make too much noise."

"Everyone hears everything here, no?"

She'd been alarmed by the noises down the air shaft—the one sound you never heard in this building was people making love.

I said nervously, "You know, I was wondering about birth control."

"It's a little late for that, isn't it?"

"I asked you a few minutes ago, remember?"

"Did you? Ah, when you asked me if it was safe!" She grinned. "In the middle of everything. I didn't know what you meant. So I said yes."

I felt the first tremors of an earthquake rattling the apartment walls before she added, "If that's what you mean, yes, it's safe. I have two of these—what do you say in English? The tiny wires."

"A coil?"

"Yes, but I have two. Before I had only one, and this is why I have Benjamin."

"I don't understand."

She said, "I have a double womb. Very rare, the doctors say. It's not dangerous or anything. But before, I didn't know. I had a coil for one but not the other. So now I have two coils and one son."

I never found out whether this was possible, or if she was making it up—at that moment I was ready to believe anything. She padded out to put the kettle on, making herself immediately at home.

Those nights were untiring: we would go from bed to shower to bed again, my windows open to let in an unseasonably warm April air and cool our bodies in the sweaty sheets. Our days were calmer. I guided her through the city, I selfishly introduced her to only a few friends, and she came to hear me play a couple of evenings in a club in Tribeca. I'd gotten subs for my other gigs that week.

It wasn't that she knew more about music than other women I'd been with, or that she was more enthusiastic about me as a musician. But both evenings I sensed her listening intently out there in the club's darkness, attuned to what I was reaching for, as if my playing was a searchlight that could find her no matter where she was hidden. I could feel her concentration following the story in each solo—hearing what there was in the music which was not music. To improvise is to live, but it is also to tell the truth without apology, and perhaps what meant the most to me is that I always felt Maja's sympathy for what I did not try to hide in my playing, all that I saw but was hesitant to say except in music.

On one of those nights, late, when we got home, I broached the subject of how she'd left things with Simon.

She said, "He took it very badly that I decided to leave. To leave and not come back. Especially that I am stopping here. He loves me, you know. But—" She took a deep breath. "I realize clear how much I love him but finally, it's not enough. No matter how much he gives me and Benjamin. And maybe one day I can love someone else more. No matter what they give me or not."

She spoke as if she didn't want to frighten me off.

I took her one day for a late lunch down on Second Avenue, at Fourth Street, to a Polish cafeteria that was a central hangout for the immigrant population. She wasn't as enthusiastic about this small surprise as I expected. Afterwards she said only that these weren't necessarily the most interesting Polacks in the world, and maybe she had a point. They did look like grumbling outcasts.

Another afternoon, back at my flat, she brought up in passing the name of a Polish illustrator she'd known years ago who'd made a career in New York. He lived only a few blocks away, according to the telephone book, and with several tries she got through. After a brief conversation in Polish, Maja hung up and said, "I gave his wife your number, but I don't think they will ring back."

"Isn't he there?"

"He's working. I remember this woman from Warsaw. She's always careful, she keeps every other woman miles away."

"Didn't you explain what you were doing here?"

"Of course. But she protects him like a tiger. We weren't great friends, anyway. He was a friend of a friend." She tried to shrug it off. "I'm sorry, I thought he would be interesting for you to meet. Doesn't matter."

Still, I saw she was exasperated that this couple didn't want to see her again, after all these years and miles. One of these days, I thought, when she visits Poland again, I'll go with her.

One morning I'd gone round the corner for some quick supplies and returned to find her glancing through photographs of old girlfriends she'd found in my dresser drawer.

She said, "You don't mind, do you? A little jealousy is good."

"You don't have any reason to be jealous."

"That's not what you're supposed to say."

"All right, who makes you jealous?"

Maja treated this as a serious question, and the photo she settled on surprised me—of a woman I'd known for barely a summer, a glittering young actress with a future. Now I saw only a professional, glycerine warmth in her face.

"This is the one I'm jealous of," Maja said with satisfaction. "And will worry about back in Amsterdam."

"You might as well worry about unicorns," I said, and took the photographs back from her.

It nagged at me, though, why she'd chosen that brief girlfriend—since it struck me that one is often most jealous of someone who reminds you most of yourself.

Her great New York enthusiasm lay in shopping for Benjamin. We spent hours in a couple of huge toy stores; for her this was like being flung into some Persian bazaar. While Maja took her time choosing among lunchboxes and schoolbags and clucking at New York prices, I wandered in amazement among interplanetary blasters and galactic robots and the computer gear that would doubtless be obsolete by the time I had a child of my own.

At some point in here my memories of her first and second visits merge, because only six weeks lay between them—she came back in early June, while Benjamin went for his annual summer visit with his grandmother in Warsaw. This time Maja stayed two weeks, settling into the pattern of my life as naturally as if we'd lived together for years. She had none of the newcomer's illusions about New York—she saw how profoundly exhausting a city it was—but she had the nomad's gift of making herself easily at home anywhere.

Or at home nowhere: I wondered how strong the need in her was to find a place she would never wish to leave. The act of trying somewhere new seemed like oxygen to her; she was utterly comfortable living out of one small traveling bag. Though Amsterdam had rescued her and her son, she hardly spoke of it as ideal.

"It's like an old, grand hotel that's lost its lucky days," she said. "So anyone can move in and live there now. That's why I love it, but when everyone around you lives in a temporary way, it doesn't inspire you to behave differently. That's not good for me."

We saw films, we walked, we made love, and one afternoon I taped her reading Milosz in Polish—I must still have the cassette somewhere. After she left I'd listen to that complex, incantatory voice, not understanding a word, and think: This is what all the nights of playing and the long years of waiting have been for, to find at last a woman with this much world in her. I would close my eyes and see her on the darkened cinema screen of my mind, moving naked about my flat: the insolent saunter of her hips as she went about some banal task, a surprised smile over her shoulder at finding me admiring her, then her confident sashay in my direction.

One evening I took her to hear Adam Makowicz, the brilliant pianist from Cracow. In his mid-forties, having emigrated a few years earlier, he'd never been acclaimed here as he deserved, partly out of sheer jealousy for his echoes of the great god Tatum. I knew him slightly—an amiable man with no pretense—from turning up so often to hear him play. A couple of years back, after praising and criticizing a demo tape I'd pressed on him, he'd asked my age. When I said twenty-five, he smiled and waggled a finger.

He said, "You have ten years. Ten years to finish to make your sound and to start to make your name. After that, it's too late."

He'd invited me to come over and play at his apartment, but I hadn't had the nerve then to take him up on the invitation. Still, I was a different player now, and Makowicz's approval might help a lot. I thought: I'll introduce him to Maja, they'll yammer away in Polish, then I'll ask him if the invitation is still open.

Makowicz was in blistering form that night, constructing his precise fantasies on tunes in a controlled theme-and-variations way. He stopped by our table in the uncrowded supper club and asked how my career was getting on. His English was improving, and with his floppy hair and lively eyes he had the enthusiasm of an eager schoolboy in a dinner jacket. I praised his playing and introduced Maja. They exchanged pleasantries in their own language, then Makowicz excused himself to speak to people at another table.

"That was quick," I muttered. "I hoped he'd join us."

"He has some close friends here, he said."

I glanced around—now Makowicz was standing at the back chatting with the manager.

"Didn't you suggest he sit down?"

"I guess he wasn't interested," she said. "There must be plenty of Polacks in New York, don't you think?"

Strange—usually he sat down without being asked and started talking about music. Once he'd compared taking a solo to building a house, adding on a wing here, a wing there, windows to let in air and light. I was convinced Maja hadn't invited him; I told myself I'd look him up after she left, though I didn't. Later I realized she was uncomfortable approaching Polacks who'd achieved greatness in the West, even though back home it would've been normal to strike up a conversation. Some old rules didn't apply in a new country.

On at least one occasion I took her in chess—I remember the satisfied gleam in her eyes as she toppled her king with a nudge of her forefinger, and how careful she was to wait a couple of days before we played again, so the victory would soak through my pores.

There were at least two new games we had not played before, that came out of a growing trust and sense of her time in New York as the first step into somewhere entirely our own. She knew I was trying to arrange a British tour for July: that was enough for the moment, the implications could remain unspoken.

The first game was one I'd never tried. I'd played a gig that night, and was drained but wide awake. We showered separately for once to get the smoke of the club off ourselves, then tumbled naked onto the sheets. A breezy night; the kitchen air shaft was alive with the feuding foreign couple three floors up.

"Lithuanian," said Maja, after listening a moment. "She says she is going to cut his throat tonight with a bread knife. After he goes to sleep." She yawned and looked sly, propped on two pillows, an unconcerned nineteenth-century nude. She said, "*Kochany*, what do you do with yourself when I'm not here?"

"You mean other women?"

"I mean in bed alone. When you think of me."

"What do you imagine? I'm sure I do more or less what you do."

"Really?" Her hand crept over to herself. "Shall I show you what I do, thinking of you? And then you show me?"

"Why?"

"Because I am sure you will like what you see. And you will know how to think of me next week when I am back in A'dam."

I was surprised by how strong, how hypnotic that game turned out to be.

And in it there was only a mutual victory. But on her last night we played a game where there was a winner and a loser.

We were lying in each other's arms, deliberately doing nothing to see, I suppose, how long we could wait, when she murmured, "Do you want to do a bet?"

"That depends."

She sat up on her knees, away from me.

She said, "I bet that I can get you interested in, oh, two minutes, without even touching you."

"How will you do that?"

"Wait and see. You must keep your eyes open. That's the only rule."

I took my wristwatch off the night table.

"Go ahead," I said. "Start when you want."

"Just a moment." She turned up the lamp, shifted on her knees to be alongside my chest. "Let's go."

I glanced at my watch's second hand, and at that instant her face appeared close to mine, humming, swaying, her eyes closed, then slowly passing across my shoulder, only an inch away, along my chest, down my stomach, lower. It took fiendish concentration to keep my eager alter ego from lancing upwards to her waiting lips. Was I going to lose so easily? I groaned as I realized that only twenty seconds had ticked away—two minutes would be an eternity.

She smiled as she saw I wasn't giving up.

She put her hands on her hips and arched backwards, her breasts proffered, her head out of sight. My eyes traced the path my hands could not, to her navel and below. All my concentration was on the difficult strategy of relaxing, and now I cannot think why in those arduous seconds I didn't realize that I should let myself lose the game easily, that to give in suddenly and pull her to me was to win, her throaty satisfied laughter was all that mattered.

Instead, with over a minute gone, she melted out of her limbo pose to broadcast a glance of determination and a confident grin. She turned on her knees, carefully straddling, with her back to me, not touching me anywhere but only by centimeters. Taunting me with what she knew I found the most tantalizing side of her. Her breath was sinuous on my thighs; I felt defeat coming on even as I watched the second hand crawl much too slowly toward the finish.

I gasped and let myself go, expecting the warm flick of her tongue followed by the hot welcome of her mouth around me. Instead she was off the complaining bed and in the other room before I had a chance to reach for her.

I heard her rummaging in her packed suitcase. When she came back she was wearing underwear.

I said, "You won, fair and square. Do I get a chance to try evening the score?"

"I don't see how. I could cheat and you'd have to trust me."

Her tone was annoyed and insulted. We argued and pretended to sleep and finally, an hour later, made love out of an instinct that we shouldn't spend what would be our last night together for a while without making love, no matter how contrived and uneasy. The point wasn't that I'd chosen to take the game seriously enough to nearly win, or that I'd misunderstood its purpose, but that I'd shown I actually could outlast such a contest. I could resist her, even when her body was pretending to be enslaved to mine, even when she was at her most irresistible. And yet the next morning I still thought she was only being a sore winner.

——————— (W A R S A W)

T he French arrived at Lena's en masse.
There were four: Yves, Anne, and
child versions of each named, appropriately, André and
Yvette. In my experience French children resemble their
parents utterly and almost politely: the rebellion usually
stays hidden.

Anne was tall and slender, a lanky blonde with a prim
mouth and the mildly disapproving air of a woman who
feels married life has let her down, and prefers the company
of other women until she can create a new face for herself.
Yves had more exuberance. He bustled in with three big
valises hanging from his shoulders and two stuffed shopping
bags that he handed over with a muttered admonition—
the bags clinked.

"*Du vin*," he said unnecessarily. He shoved straggly
black hair out of his eyes and began extricating himself from
his family's baggage. Cheese was in there somewhere,

highly dubious after a train journey that the women were already discussing in two languages. The children, who might've been six and seven, wandered about the flat hunting for a toilet.

In minutes the children were marched obediently off to bed up in the loft just outside the room where Maja and I slept, and the three women began reverently unwrapping and rewrapping mountainous stinking slabs of cheese and cooing over them like pigeons.

It didn't seem to bother Yves that my French was only roadworthy up to about thirty kilometers an hour. He winked at me, said, *"Viens,"* and motioned me to join him at the long table.

His accent was heavily Marseilles, where he owned a small construction company. A cigarette hung precariously from a corner of his mouth; as if by prestidigitation a corkscrew materialized in his hand. He began setting out wines and babbling away about their pedigrees or how he'd gotten them cheap from the vintner's cousin. He alerted me right away that we'd call each other by the familiar form of "you." I asked him to excuse that I simply used whichever form came out first. It was good to have another man around. He and I sat at one end of the long table, the women at the other.

Lena's dominion in the flat, which Maja challenged whenever guests arrived, was restored by Anne's arrival; now Lena could be the elder these two had in common. Plans for the two days before Christmas, involving Benjamin and the two French children, were suggested in French, modified in Polish, approved again in French.

I was trying to explain to Yves that the Poles celebrated Christmas dinner on the eve of the twenty-fourth before I realized the French did so as well and I was only confusing him.

He said, "So she's yours, eh? What's her name again? Inca?"

"Maja. We're living in Amsterdam. But it's not sure."

"You're American, right? What kind of business? Export?"

"Jazz music. The clarinet."

"You know, I'm crazy about jazz. I really love the old jazz. Sidney Bechet, you know? Django Reinhardt? Ben Webster? Stéphane Grappelli? The modern stuff is intellectual crap, if you ask me. I can't play a note, but I don't give a shit. I hate these people who say they play and they fall on their ass when you ask them to play three notes of the Marseillaise. They should keep their mouths shut and listen to a genius. You a genius?"

"I can play more than three notes."

He rubbed his face with the back of his arm. "Shit, what a train ride. What kind of a country is this, anyway? I tried to buy some vodka on the train, they didn't have any in the bar. Just cherry juice or some crap like that. I said: Listen, we crossed the border into Poland already, right? So where's the famous vodka? I wanted the one with the buffalo hair in it, it's supposed to be the best, they make you cough up a fortune for it in Paris. Maybe I'll start importing myself if the margin's interesting. But not by train. Next time, I drive—" He made a gesture of swift escape with one hand. He sighed. "She's contented now, but you should've heard my wife on the train. Complaining like a donkey. Is it my fault the Soviets can't make this railroad run on time?"

An hour later we'd finished two bottles and turned in. I was slightly sparked, intoxicated more by the effort of having to speak French with someone new than by the wine. With another couple there it was easier to feel part of a couple alongside Maja. Usually after these evenings with the Polish horde, outnumbered and outtalked, I'd crawl under the blankets with her like a weary exile.

I wasn't practicing much, either, and this left me feeling I'd abandoned myself—it's easy, once discipline slips and you're depressed, to slip further. I was playing only enough to be able to say I'd picked up the instrument that day, not enough to maintain my chops or my self-respect.

So that evening as I slid under the sleeping bag on that hard mattress beside Maja, who already had her back turned, I vowed: I'm going to attack her once and for all. The four, five days we'd been here she'd managed to be asleep almost immediately and would murmur a no whenever I began to touch her. Left to it, she'd do nothing, apparently—it was up to me.

Buried under a synthetic sleeping bag that was our only choice against the drafts that occasionally found their way in, it seemed unbelievable how the world could be so frozen outside and yet so stifling inside this back room. The sleeping bag's weight kept us clammy all night; nothing sensual or tender about sleeping this way. It seemed natural to maintain a distance between our underclothed bodies and keep our sweat to ourselves. Tonight, as if sensing my intentions, she wore one of my T-shirts as well.

Could it be that Lena's flat had particular memories that were intruding? Or was it because, back in her home country, she felt she no longer had a place of her own, having chosen to make a life and raise her son in another culture? She rarely mentioned Benjamin even to old friends except when they asked after him. He was obviously enjoying the experience of being away from Mama to be spoiled by grandparents, but this was also a way to avoid reminding her friends that she was old enough to have a nine-year-old boy. Without him underfoot she could still preserve the illusion of an eternal youthfulness, because she really did look in her twenties.

Lying beside her body's warmth, her backside turned to me, I could propose anything I liked, but months of separation had dislocated us. When I'd left her in late September in Amsterdam, having flown over for ten days, we were both flush with the idea of my joining her for good. But many weeks of expectant letters and impatient phone calls had sapped all our bravado and giddiness and most of her desire. What was so romantic about an American who made you wait three months before finally coming to join you out of sheer headlong passion?

People say there is nothing more mysterious than friendship, but friendship survives long after desire, and doesn't depend on the weather or telephoning at the right moment. I don't understand how easily desire drips away, how quickly it evaporates in the desert.

She had, I'm fairly sure, had an affair—at least a night or two with someone else—before I joined her. She'd hinted as much, and I'd certainly said a midnight good-bye to an old girlfriend in New York, so it didn't seem worth discussing. What mattered was that we pick up again as if it were only a week and not months since we'd last tumbled away from each other, exhausted by an afternoon in tangled sheets. If love from her body wasn't there in a home country she'd deliberately fled, it still didn't necessarily mean the feeling between us was lost, only that it was up to me to awaken it.

Determined tonight, I wasn't coaxing, or subtle—an approach I'd tried fruitlessly on different nights that week. I simply snaked my way down and went after her with my mouth, teasing her through her underwear. I'd several times brought her to squirming oblivion this way, without even pulling off her cotton underpants; tonight she gave an angry flip of her body and turned aside. It is astonishing how many miles broad a barren mattress can feel.

I knew I would get nowhere by letting her be the stronger; having laid down a challenge, I had to carry it all the way. This game too we'd played in the past, to great mutual satisfaction, so I pulled her to my mouth again, the sleeping bag bunched around us, and began making my way up her.

"No."

I hadn't gotten very far.

"No."

When I persisted she grabbed my hair with one hand— no matter what your determination, this will make you cease and desist.

I grabbed her wrist and flung it away. She gave a little laugh and hugged her knees to her chest.

"What is it you want?" she said in an amused whisper—not wishing to rouse the French family sleeping, all four together, not fifteen feet away on the other side of a door.

"What do you think I want?" I added a sentence which had once thrilled us both but now, in my harsh whisper, tasted as futile as any obscenity.

"You think this is the way?" she said.

"I guess not. I've tried every way I can think of. You tell me."

She seemed entertained by the situation. "Why make it easy?"

"Then you get to enjoy yourself also. Maybe it's an old-fashioned idea."

"But I'm enjoying this. I don't know why you think wrestling is a good way to get a woman to make love. You weren't always so obvious."

"I give up," I said. "This isn't an interesting game. We

can't move forward in this way, if you make me fight to stay in the same place. It's not worth it."

"I'm not worth it?" she said. "Do you think this is the way to make me more interested? I thought I am the best you ever had, you told me so a hundred times. Now you change your opinion when you think it will help you."

"I don't understand. Does it make you feel better to treat me this way?"

She said, "You *don't* understand. I simply don't want to make love with you now."

I didn't say a word.

"Before, I thought about you day and night."

"So what changed?"

I felt her shift in the darkness. "Maybe I got tired of wanting you in A'dam and waiting for you. So I used up years and years of desire, of wanting you to make love with me, but you were never there. And now I find someone else."

"Who?"

She said, "Oh, I don't know. No one, yet. Or who knows, maybe it comes back from your direction, and tomorrow I change my mind about wanting you again. I'm sorry to have to explain all this to you, I thought you would realize on your own."

"I did realize."

"I can't apologize because it's not my fault. I don't say it's yours, either. And if you want to leave, I understand. Or if you want to stay and see what happens, that's all right. But I don't promise anything, and if I meet someone else, I don't hold back because you are still here. That's the risk we take. Or maybe you meet someone else."

"I moved to Europe because of you. I didn't come to back down if there's a problem."

"You didn't come here only because of me," she said.

"Anyway, a problem is something that you hold in your hands. I'm speaking of what's missing, and you can't whistle to bring it back. The best thing for us would be for you to go away for a time."

"I thought that was the problem."

How earnest, how well-meaning: I was offering to duplicate Simon's strategy. I almost wish I could run into him today, to tell him I came to know how he must have felt, to understand why he treated Maja with distance and even spoke combatively with her in front of strangers. The man had only been trying to keep his head above water—to keep swimming and survive.

"But now I've seen you again," she said. "Why don't you go with Wojciech to Cracow? And look for grandfather for a few days. I'll stay here. Perhaps I'll miss you. If I get crazy homesick for you before Wojciech returns, any day you can come back by train."

I saw the drawbacks of following her suggestion (though Cracow had been my idea, from the start) along with the possibility that she was right, this was all it might take.

I said, "And if I decide I don't want to bother I can simply fly direct back to Holland. From Cracow."

"If you like."

"When is Wojciech leaving?"

"Christmas Day. But you must come back by the last day of the year. For this costume party, we can't miss it." She snapped her fingers. "I must remind Lena tomorrow to get tickets for the French delegation. The promoters will run out of tickets soon, you'll see."

As if tickets were the question of paramount importance.

She said, "You see how relaxed Yves is? Those two are almost certainly going to divorce, Lena tells me. Still he keeps his sense of humor. *This* is very attractive in a man— he doesn't bother whether you leave him or not. He acts as if everything is funny, he doesn't care what you think. This makes you want to stay with him."

I said, "So who are the other women I should meet?"

"You should concentrate on Zosia. In my opinion." Maja sounded sincere. "She's by herself. She looks very interested, I think."

I couldn't see Maja's face in the darkness, and I was glad she couldn't see mine, as I feigned a casual indifference to whether we stayed lovers or not, pretending to consider coolly the possibility of Zosia, speaking in this disarming worldly way as if poison weren't spreading through my limbs.

With that truce we turned our backs on each other. She was soon fast asleep, but I could not slow my mind's whirling. Outside there was no starlight. I'd drunk too much; a few times in the interminable night I got up to relieve myself silently in the paint-stained sink. When I finally slept, with those apocalyptic science fiction paintings all around me in darkness, it was to dream I was walking beside Maja in a futuristic nuclear wasteland where—even in the dream I could feel it coming—we rounded a grotesque corner, and abruptly I stood alone in an empty, burned-out city.

After so many months imagining Maja's life in Holland with her son, it had been a shock, in July sunlight, after a week of serious club work in London with my guitarist friend Stan, and a gradual arrival by ferry and train, to see how they actually lived.

Their flat was sublet—borrowed, really, for Maja owed many months' back rent—from a Dutch friend, a doctor who now lived with his girlfriend. His name was Otto van Poppen, and he was as beleaguered as his name, divorced from a Polish wife he was still madly in love with and who'd taken their daughter off to Italy years earlier. He was still paying the bills and occasionally going south for a repri-manding Tuscan visit.

Maja explained all this as she showed me the little flat—comfortable for one, feasible for two, probably asking too much of three. Benjamin had his room (the daughter's, once) off a hallway. Facing it was a small study that Doctor

Otto came in to use from time to time, crammed with books in a dozen languages and a single mattress on the floor for guests. The only large room was in back, a dining table at one end, a television and armchairs at the other. Here Maja and I unrolled a futon every night, fitted it with sheets, and slept until Benjamin woke us getting his morning cereal.

The flat shocked me not because it was cheerless or small, for it was also spotless, modern, and in a new suburb of Amsterdam near a small park, much nicer than where I lived in New York. But I suddenly saw their days, their future, as unchanging as a photograph. No wonder Maja needed constant motion, to keep away the fear that this was what her life might be for the next decade, until she was in her forties and Benjamin went off to university. Small wonder she'd been willing to try Port Stilton until the bitter end, and to see what might happen with an American musician she barely knew.

"You give me the improvising back," she told me once. "I lost it for too long. This time I hold on to that feeling with both hands. Because nothing matters as much to me."

It sounds silly, but I walked into their flat, felt my own small place in New York reverberate back at me, and vowed that together we would come up with something better. A person with Maja's spirit and instincts deserved a place of her own, deserved a life appropriate to the adventure she could bring to an innocent swim or an overseas correspondence, the sense of risk she'd shown leaving Poland. I was on the verge of making a mark with my music, I could feel it; I'd been composing tunes for a record, I had a freshening sense that all was possible. Maja's presence had aligned my life in a way that my professional discipline hadn't ordered it before. Perhaps it came from knowing that, had I been offering any less of myself, she would not bother with me.

We had an easy week together. She hadn't yet found work, she had a bit of money saved up from what the Dutch government had been giving her, the doctor was undemanding about the rent; Benjamin was on holiday so he often joined his schoolfriends for the day. If he stayed home he listened to me practice while solemnly constructing interplanetary launching pads and gyroscopic space stations. He'd be in his room, I across the hallway in the doctor's study, Maja cooking beef stroganoff in my honor or doing yoga with the television on—a background buzz that, instead of breaking my concentration, made me feel part of an instantaneous family.

Most evenings we went out. Amsterdam had a great range of exotic restaurants, and we could choose Indonesian or Brazilian or Haitian ("Never Polish," she insisted) simply by crossing an arched, gaily lit bridge. The canals stank, but the city of gingerbread row houses was compact, knowable, and alert. It made New York seem terribly out of control.

If I hadn't had gigs to get back to I'd have stayed on, and by now we found ourselves discussing the possibility almost as a mutual dare. She was careful to take me one night to a little club off the Leidseplein where I sat in with a strong tenor player from Manchester. He'd come over from England a decade earlier; as he pointed out, Amsterdam would give me a firm foothold on the continent. Brussels was three hours away by train, Paris six, London a ferry; there was always work in Germany, and more jazz festivals in Europe than in the States. I wouldn't be the first American jazzer to make a better name here than was feasible back home. Anyway, New York no longer felt much like home.

For all Maja's encouragement of my music, her sense of that very difficult professional world was limited. She knew a few Polish musicians who'd made a slight name for themselves outside Eastern Europe, but she didn't appreciate the competition I was up against in the States, or how difficult it was simply to get your tapes listened to by major booking agents or record companies. Sometimes I felt that she thought I was weaving excuses; I doubt she understood how tenuous the work was in the first place, nor the connections I'd be letting go slack to join her.

One afternoon Maja announced, "I have a surprise for you." She took me by tram to a run-down section of the city and led me up a rickety flight of stairs above a bar full of yelling football fans. The blonde who greeted us from behind a heavy door was wearing very little—a crisscross of flesh-colored brassiere that showed her aureoles plainly and a similar scrap of underpants.

She and Maja launched into a barrage of hugs and Polish banter. She eyed me appraisingly over Maja's shoulder, said hello in a marauding way and kissed me boldly on the mouth. She wheeled and swung into her vault, and as I followed the bouncing ball, Maja said mildly, "I think I warned you about Saskia."

Saskia made us tea before she conceded it might be a good idea if she got dressed. Her ramshackle flat was an enormous loft space with high windows, evidently designed for a turn-of-the-century painter. One end was cluttered with wood planks and rusted machine parts, as it'd been a factory for decades. Mostly, though, there were Saskia's paintings, hung right round the walls.

These were almost too gigantic to take in. I can't say if they were good or not. They were intentional—she knew what she was doing—and usually abstract, full of color on an epic scale. I gazed at her canvases and wondered what they would lose by being shrunk to quarter-size. They'd certainly be easier to hang in a gallery, sell, and take home.

I said as much to Maja while Saskia was changing at the far end of the loft.

"That's what I think, too," said Maja. "But the more you say this, the bigger her paintings get. Tell her, it will be good for her to hear it from a stranger."

"I don't want to be the one. She might throw a radio at me, like she did with the Javanese bouncer."

Just then Saskia appeared and began telling us earnestly about her boyfriend in New York. She had a photo of him somewhere, she'd find it. He was a journalist, he was too skinny, his parents both disapproved of her, they had all the money, but she didn't care if they were poor together; he said if they got married his parents would disinherit him but if they had a child they'd re-inherit him; she wasn't sure he loved her for herself, without her paintings; she'd had a brief affair with a black bartender in a nightclub here and wondered if she should tell her boyfriend in New York, since it might worry him. Most important, she didn't see why he couldn't persuade a Soho gallery to give her a one-woman show.

From her paintings and from her underwear Saskia seemed like a lot of woman to deal with.

I asked how she could transport such large canvases. She said to Maja in her broken English, "You see? Your American is not dreamer, like mine. He is practical-minded. He sees problem, he looks for solution. I think your American is better than my American." She put her arm around me, laid her head affectionately on my shoulder, and said, "I will keep."

"You would kill each other in five minutes," said Maja.

Saskia detached herself to show us several slide sheets of her work that included, not incidentally, some shots of herself nude and paint-spattered, lying across large red and yellow canvases. I never know what to say about someone's art when it's clear they only want all the adoration you have to give—better to pretend you see eye-to-eye with them against an uninitiated world. This was clearly Maja's strategy, and I adopted it.

"Don't you need to lose a couple of kilos, my little rabbit?" said Maja, holding a sheet of transparencies to the light.

"Don't you wish, my little rabbit," said Saskia, "you had all that I have to lose?"

Now she was pulling out boxes of higgledy-piggledy old photos of Poland, and there, in fading black and white among many worn Saskias, were several Majas I'd never seen before. A school jaunt in the countryside, heavy-eyed in girlish makeup. Naked and full-bellied in profile, pregnant with Benjamin. Slim again, young and at peace, nude, a baby foot poking out of the shadows beside her.

Eventually the two women's English broke down and the slow afternoon dissipated into wine and Polish chatter. I wandered among the paintings and put on some Mahler and took my time looking through the photos. How proper the people seemed in these Polish snapshots of fifteen years ago, before everyone became hippies and looked smoked-out and weary. Maja always managed to appear exceptional. No matter how she praised them, these other Polish women didn't have her allure, her blowtorch gaze, her promise.

Every once in a while the two women would glance at me and dissolve into fits of laughter. Occasionally Saskia shot me a knowing wink that reminded me of her other line of work, and made me wonder about the dancing Maja had mentioned months ago in Port Stilton.

That night Maja and I ate alone; Benjamin was staying at a schoolmate's. She asked me what I thought of Saskia.

"I liked her. But you didn't tell me you danced in the peep show with her."

She grinned a little guiltily over her soup.

"That's the dancing you did when you came from Warsaw, right?"

"I only worked there a year."

"It doesn't bother me. You could've told me."

"I'm glad it doesn't bother you," she said. "If it did I'd ask you to leave. I didn't tell you a story. Well," she admitted, "not really. That's how I met Simon. He was managing a café around the corner where the other girls and I went for our coffees."

Instead of being hurt in retrospect by her lie, or rather her careful misleading, I was flattered—even early on she'd been concerned with what I might think of her.

"So what was it like?"

"It isn't what you think, the peep show. If you have a look you'll see the Dutches keep their massage and the heavy business separate. Saskia and I used to laugh at the men staring at us as soon as they went away. They looked like fishes with big eyes."

Drowning from looking at you, I thought.

"So you danced naked all day long? It must've been tiring."

"You don't dance all the time," said Maja. "They had us in our own little room, Saskia and I. When a man paid to come in he had to go down a little tunnel to where he could see us. A bell would ring to tell us to start the music and dance. So we were sitting around talking most of the time. Then if the man liked us he would put money directly in a slot and we would dance a little more." She paused. "It's not easy to do well, you know."

"I'm sure it's not."

There is probably no more discriminating audience anywhere, I thought, than a solitary guy in a raincoat.

"Listen, there are beautiful girls here. The men come to a peep show because they know they can find *you* there after work or during lunch. If they like you they slip you more money or they write you letters sometimes. But if they don't like you they go on to someone else. I did very well, I almost never had any trouble. Saskia and I were very popular because we would do anything people wanted together."

"Anything?"

"Not *really* anything," said Maja. "We would pretend. When they're peeping through a window they can't tell the difference. But sometimes Saskia would surprise me. Most of the time we were doing sexy faces and trying not to giggle. If you laughed the man knew you were laughing at him, and he'd complain to the Javanese and never come back."

It is not a question of who you are but of who you are capable of becoming when you have no other choice. Maja had turned into a nude dancer, this was what I'd seen in her walk and enjoyed in bed. It was all too easy to glimpse her, stripped and undulating, through the small window of my imagination. Perhaps she didn't mind having men pay to look at her naked so long as her documents were properly in order. What would I turn myself into under similar circumstances? I could not imagine myself realistically as a refugee, or an exile, or someone who'd gotten away—whatever it was she was. I wasn't sure what she was.

And yet I used to joke with fellow musicians about being all these things: what was jazz if not a way out, a means of escape? Escape certainly fed a profound hunger. Wasn't this really what my professional life added up to? She knew better than I ever could what escape might mean, and how much a person could come to live in that longing.

Later in the evening, she asked suddenly, "Do you think Saskia wants to sleep with you?"

I wondered if she really meant it the other way around. "Does Saskia normally dress like that in front of strangers?"

"She got used to it," said Maja. "You can imagine."

I didn't think Maja took Saskia's flirtations seriously. But that night in bed she wouldn't let me do anything—she was fiercer and more giving than ever—and afterwards she sang softly to me, that same chromatic Polish melody but wordless this time, until I slid holding her into sleep.

_____ (CRACOW)

It was dark on Christmas Day when Wojciech and I and the battered Mercedes emerged from the fog just north of Cracow. In moonlight the snow lay on the fields like a clotted creamy borscht. Occasionally we passed beneath a concrete bridge over the highway, and the weak headlights would glance at the mottos painted on broad signs hung from the bridge's underbelly—COMMUNIST PEOPLES ARE MOVING FORWARD, CAPITALIST PEOPLES MOVING BACKWARDS and similar inspiring thoughts, according to my poet-driver's translation.

"One day," he said cheerfully, "all sign will be antique. Soviet Army leave, *poof!* In one hour, you don't find a sign like this anywhere."

The outskirts of the city were a few villages, more mechanized than others we'd passed. Cracow was upon us in a welter of housing developments, like those immense ghosts I'd walked among looking for ghosts of my grandfather.

Then we were hurrying down slick dark boulevards with balconied buildings intact from the last century—not the imposing, imprisoning edifices of a capital but smaller, more humane. They reminded me that Cracow had never been bombed, not once.

It was only eight, but no one was about: except for the odd lighted window of a café (quaint curtains, the veiled flicker of a fireplace within) Cracow seemed deserted, stilled by clumps of snow drifted in its somber doorways. We came to a belt of park beside medieval battlements. The joined houses bordering the trees and grass were larger and older, Liszt or even Mozart era; few lights showed. Wojciech parked, sighed, and patted the steering wheel. Quickening footsteps faded. It was snowing again.

"So, American, welcome to Cracow," said Wojciech. "From here, you don't mind I hope, we walk."

I had only one bag, but Wojciech was laden with packages for his sons and ex-mistress. We divided the load and headed down shadowy streets made more alien by strands of fog and a few weary street lamps. I felt I was walking through an antique painting, into an old elegant world abused, brought low, by weather.

We turned into an arched black doorway and mounted steep stone stairs, Wojciech cursing the lack of light. On a second-floor landing he hammered on a carved wooden door and shouted something jovial. There were running footsteps, a bolt shot back, and he was embraced by two boys leaping like puppies.

A dark-haired woman, beautiful in a rather severe and refined way, ushered me in. "Excuse me, I am Vera. We are very worried, you are never here. Welcome."

Her flat, despite its old skin (sixteenth century, she said) was as modern as money in Poland could buy: white walls, track lighting, sleek Scandinavian furniture, and an expensive Japanese stereo. Posters for rock concerts in Germany and France were framed in the hallway, but they were the only sign that Vera was a rock star, at least in Eastern European terms. She seemed more like the concerned housewife of an overworked executive. Her affection for Wojciech was reserved and proper, as if she didn't want him to get any old ideas.

Tea was already made. Afterwards, they showed me to one of the boys' narrow bedrooms (posters of European athletes on the walls), surrendered on my behalf. I felt I should leave the family to catch up, not force them into a polite difficult conversation in English. So I excused myself and said I wanted to get some air and no, I didn't get easily lost. Neither was true, but I went down and out into Cracow's streets again.

I was immediately overcome by a suffocating dizziness. I didn't know these people, I was their guest on Christmas Night in a strange old city dreaming among stone shadows and snow, I could feel Maja slipping inexorably through my fingers, what was I supposed to do? Where was I supposed to go in all this fog? Every old street looked the same, lined with its gloomy patriarchs shut tight against the mists, with its wrong turnings misleading you back always to the same corner.

I began to wonder what of me still survived here. I didn't feel much like anyone anymore, I was just another anonymous man in Poland walking around and aimlessly talking himself into the night. What could I resurrect in this fog of who I was, where I had been? Fog was normal here, the natural state of affairs, so already I'd learned to fit in. People averted their faces as I passed—or it might've been that they simply didn't notice one more figure in the mists. My overcoat huddled around my ears, my eyes smarting and weeping from the cold, I thought: I came all this way to prove to myself that I don't exist? I am going to dissolve.

I'd been letting the street of distant centuries lead me. No lamps showed anywhere, and this utter absence of human light on Christmas only increased my sensation of eeriness, until I came to the end of the street. Without warning I found myself on the verge of a great medieval square with a long arcaded hall in the center, a squat bulbous church ahead, and a tall Gothic church of uneven steeples near me, pouring light from a doorway onto people waiting to get in; and from it flowed the pure transparent voices of Gregorian chant, plaintively echoing about the square.

I let myself be led to the sound, and stood outside with the others, listening. I felt too enveloped in solitude to want to go in and be part of a worshipping throng. Their dominion of faith could never be mine, but even standing here in the faint snowfall with these others listening, smoking or shifting their feet nervously to keep warm, I could feel its strength, the beauty of something believed, rolling a thread of song past us and back around the square, holding us with an open melody in the eighth mode, so clear in feeling that it was the chant's measured lyricism which brought tears to my eyes, and not my own confusion.

I still have this in me, I thought, I can still connect with it outside of me. I am not lost. Nearly lost but not yet.

Two Poles could bring a military air to an otherwise flexible day. The elaborate strategy for the afternoon involved the men and women going on separate campaigns. Yves and his son André and I would head off by ourselves, with me leading the way through this city I supposedly knew so well; Lena and Maja would take Anne and Yvette shopping, since the stores would be drained of merchandise after Christmas. We'd all meet by the old palace in Lazienki Park.

Yves seemed perfectly content with this arrangement, though I warned him I didn't know my way around.

"Who cares if we find the women?" he said. "Let them look for us. We'll have a good lunch, a good wine, it's snowing, my son is happy. That's enough."

His son clasped his hand resolutely. When we crossed the great boulevard of Marszalkowska Street the boy, at Yves's curt instructions, obediently took my hand as well.

I still hadn't solved the problem of what to take Maja's family tomorrow night—with the exception of a lone bottle of champagne for Lena, thoughtlessly I'd come here without Christmas presents for anyone but Benjamin and Maja. She'd made it clear I was expected to give something. Even chocolates, so mundane back in Amsterdam, would be appropriate. My only hope was to brave the lines at one of the Pewex shops, the government stores that sold Western goods—Johnny Walker whiskey and Eveready batteries and Parisian lingerie—in return for dollars, francs, or marks. A preposterous situation: it was against the law for Poles to buy foreign currency, yet legal for them to keep it in bank accounts. All a government racket to get the black market working for them.

In a snow falling ever faster I led us to the main Pewex, with faceless wood panelling that seemed the socialist notion of swank. You weren't allowed to handle merchandise yourself. A stone-faced shrew, peeved you might be buying something, plonked down the item and monitored you sourly while you decided if you really wanted it.

I realized afterwards that this was only Warsaw's way— in Cracow you carried on a little extended love affair with the shopgirls before money changed hands, then you were sadly out of their lives forever, replaced by the next lucky customer.

The Pewex merchandise was shelved in an accidental parody of the Western way of life. Socks were next to, say, potato chips, flashbulbs next to underwear, wine alongside laundry detergent, tinned pineapples next to basketball sneakers. The prices, cited in dollars, were normal by American standards; at an official rate of exchange they wouldn't have amounted to much in *zlotys*. But since Poles were condemned to shop here with hard currency bought on the black market, it made a tube of toothpaste into the equivalent of a twenty-dollar investment, and blue jeans into a month's wages.

"Pirates," said Yves, once I managed to unravel all this in my cumbersome French. He winced at the procedure for actually buying chocolate bars and a bottle of Scotch. Forms were reluctantly filled out by one shrew, payment made at the other end of the shop to another shrew, the purchases picked up elsewhere from a third, the forms vindictively stamped and initialed and stamped again with final annoyance by the shrew at the door.

"If I lived here," said Yves solemnly, "I would bomb such stores all the way to the devil."

The boy was getting hungry, so we stopped in at a small restaurant, done in tired linoleum and dingy green wallpaper, with the heat turned up high to counteract the blast of air from the Russian steppe whenever the door jangled open.

It was an education to watch a Frenchman savor a bottle of Bulgarian wine. Yves eyed it suspiciously, sluiced it around his glass, breathed it in with deep distrust, sipped, then brightened. He said, "So what about the Polish women? They're not so beautiful, I think."

"You might change your mind after we walk a little more."

"Maybe. With this diet, no wonder they get fat. Potatoes and more potatoes. Stew, sausage, cabbage, over and over. Look how fast these guys shovel it down. They can't wait to get back in the snow. Your friend's got a boy too, no?"

"That's right. But he's not mine."

"Don't you want another of your own? I recommend it. Makes you grow up too quickly, though."

I said, "I don't think we'll get the chance," and choked on the lumpen beef stew. If it was beef.

"Never mind. You have to learn to laugh when they

leave you. It's the only thing that makes them want to come back."

We both clammed up when his son asked if there was any dessert.

The snow had continued to accelerate, and it was exhilarating to walk through its settling hush to the occasional clank and wheeze of a tram, or the muddy cough of one of those local toy-cars stumbling along. Winter was the true ruler of Warsaw: its brightness made the elegant old buildings which had survived the war shine. On this boulevard of magisterial houses turned into embassies, the symbol of the city, a mermaid with a sword and shield, came at me from every other eave.

It seems a long time ago now, but when I think back on Poland it is, strangely, that walk in the snow with the French father and son which I remember first. Perhaps because the memory has little to do with Maja, perhaps I was touched by the genteel grandeur of those once-private family mansions now at the service of foreign governments—Swiss, Mongolian, Bulgarian. And the long-haired mermaid brandishing her blade against the onslaught of winter.

Lazienki Park edged the boulevard: oaks, hedges, formal gardens snowed in, a statue of Chopin looking trapped. Stone steps descended to a larger stretch of park, like a king's wood in olden days, where people strolled with reverence among huge trees, always wearing the grand coats and fur hats that seemed the protection of a richer people. I was in my long black woolen coat, bought at a Soho secondhand shop years ago, its capacious pockets filled with the morning's purchases, so I walked armored by chocolate and whiskey against the cold. On benches lining the paths elderly couples sat in clusters, not speaking, waiting for Christmas and grandchildren beneath a smudged sky.

Among bony trees by an observatory, stone lions lay asleep.

Yves said, "Isn't that your friend? The tall one with the boy?"

Maja greeted Yves and André and me with equal enthusiasm; she said the other three "girls" were by the lake. Benjamin towed a sled given him a few days early by Maja's father. I was glad the boy wasn't staying with us at Lena's— he'd have surely sensed, if he hadn't already back in Amsterdam, how badly Maja and I were getting along.

At first the two boys, realizing they had no language in common, stared each other down defiantly; then they were sniffing at each other like dogs; in a moment they were tumbling down a snowy slope with shrieks that made the old folks on the benches look over at us.

Yves excused himself to go watch the boys.

Maja and I walked in silence through the shushing snow until we came to an Italianate palace of faded stone, ornately columned, with statues on the roof balustrades. By the courtyard of iron lamps the motionless lake looked enameled. Statues of nude women cavorted on urns and pedestals, playing at love.

"In the spring these trees are lilacs," said Maja. "It's a shame you can't see it then in blooming. Like blue fire."

Beneath a little arched bridge the lake was frozen; flotillas of ducks patrolled the edges of the ice, and swans rose from the water to shake out their feathers on the courtyard stones.

"I can imagine," I said.

The summer palace of dead kings, the lake, the couples strolling—all had a perilous, enchanted beauty, preserved as if under a sleeping-spell from another century. No wonder Poles came here, to remind themselves of who they used to be.

I said, "You must've walked here often."

"All the times. When we were small, with our parents. Then my girlfriends and I. Then with boyfriends."

"Ever with an American?"

"You're the first," she said. "An English, once. We heard a Chopin concert, I think."

Beside the palace, a peacock shivered and fanned his tail.

"I'm sorry the palace is closed today," said Maja. "You should come another time and see how Stanislaw lived. Our last king, more than two centuries back."

"It's still intact inside?"

"All restored. It looked like bits of bread when the Germans were finished. We hid most of the treasures during the war, but the Nazis found the Rembrandts. They've still got them, somewhere."

She spoke scornfully. Just then Yves came up, breathless, with the boys straggling behind, Benjamin dragging the sled as André guided it.

"This place looks like a baby Versailles," murmured Yves.

"Merlini," said Maja. "Italian architect." She understood enough French. "Once Warsaw was like Paris, eh? Not so long ago."

She cast me a deliberate look and I translated. Yves nodded. He said by way of apology, "Absolutely. Don't think I didn't notice that formidable boulevard back there."

Benjamin said to me in his purling English, "Don't you want to take us sledding?"

"Sure. You choose the spot. Don't hit any old ladies."

"We won't hit any old people at all," he promised.

"No, no," said Yves. "Don't worry, I'll stay with them until the other women show up." He trudged off again behind the boys, who were already scampering and squealing up a slope down which other sleds jounced. Fathers stood around, bored or proud, as their long afternoon entered a single memory of many snowfalls, many Sundays, that would gather over the years.

Maja said indifferently, "Did you ask Yves to keep leaving us alone so you can talk to me?"

"Of course not."

"I told you, the best thing you can do is make me miss you. Not be standing around me all the time."

"Well, I'm going to Cracow. I'll let you know how I feel after I get there."

"What does this mean?"

I felt ready to assassinate her.

"It means I might settle down there and teach clarinet for a few months for ten *zlotys* an hour. Just to see if you miss me. Because any suffering is worthwhile if it accomplishes that, right?"

"Now you're angry," she said with delight. "I've never seen an American angry. Except your Hollywood president when he speaks of the Kremlin. But I think you're angrier than he is." She stroked my cheek once, a brief loving gesture. "You're going to teach those Cracow girls in short dresses to play the clarinet? Must I be jealous?"

"Go drown in the lake," I said, and headed off across the stone courtyard past the swans, shaking with rage. I must've passed Yves and the boys sledding and perhaps even Lena and Anne and her little Yvette, but I didn't notice.

Before I knew it I was leaving the snowy park and Chopin behind, stomping back along the avenue of embassies. It must've been four by then, the afternoon already sullen with evening, lamps damply glowing in the curtained cafés. Where was I going? I wouldn't be able to get back into Lena's flat until the others returned. I also knew I didn't want to cram myself in a crowded tram to the Old Square.

An *antikwariat* saved me, its windows luminous with old books and framed prints and the promise of unplumbed treasures within. The elderly husband and wife proprietors took my coat and gave me tea while I took my time among stacks of Soviet magazines from the fifties showing busty girls toiling on tractors, and Polish fashion magazines from the thirties showing well-dressed couples on lakeside terraces. I found a German pocket score from Leipzig, of Wagner's *Siegfried Idyll*—and sipping tea, letting the warmth of the old bookshop suffuse me, I paged through it slowly, hearing the music swell in my skull, feeling it restore me, one magnificent harmonic suspension sliding into another until I felt my calmer self again.

I don't know what the proprietors thought, watching me: a man listening to the music in his head looks not entranced but shell-shocked, stunned at what he thinks he hears. At a certain point I quietly closed Wagner and put the score back on the shelf, like a lucky talisman for someone else to find. In the end I bought a small bookplate from the twenties in a handsome darkwood frame. It showed a naked woman seated on the edge of a canopied bed, looking very winsome. She has put the book she was reading face down on the bed, because an enormous lobster, antennae waving, perched on the floor, is pinching her delectable legs in his claws. I wasn't sure what it meant, but it seemed like a dream I wished I'd had.

It was night by the time I left the *antikwariat*. I walked, enjoying the exercise now. The snow had ceased, and the city at last glistened and gleamed, even though it was poorly lit to save electricity.

At one of the tourist hotels I bought yesterday's *Herald Tribune*, its front page full of the Reagan family's Christmas plans. Over a high-priced goulash I read about nuclear negotiations with the Soviets, and thought: Suppose Maja and

I can't resolve anything? Do I go back to New York? Start over, at triple the rent I was paying a month ago?

Luckily the newspaper lasted me through most of the goulash, because once I started to think, I couldn't eat, and began to feel dizzy, as if on the ragged edge of a flu.

I bought an approved Poland guidebook at the hotel kiosk and sat in the bar, reading. Under "Nightlife" the guidebook mentioned a jazz club called the Akwarium, and listed as regulars a few Polish jazz greats who hadn't defected, like Tomas Stanko, and my man (her man) Rzupinski.

The jazz club was only a few blocks from Lena's flat. I paid my bar bill and set off wandering again.

It was barely nine-thirty when I found the Akwarium. I'd thought the music might just be starting; I didn't have my clarinet, though I could always nip back to the flat and pick it up. That would salvage the evening, at least.

There was only a lone couple chatting at a corner table and a concerned man leaning against the bar. I saw no stage and asked him about the music; he pointed upstairs. I found a good-sized room with the black walls and bleak mood that used to be the decor of all clubs—back in the days when jazz was considered serious social commentary, which here it probably still was. But the tables were empty, an unlit candle on each, and the piano on the raised stage in a dark corner was shut.

I asked the man downstairs, now behind the bar, when the music would be starting. I noticed the couple had left.

He was blond, with a trim beard and mustache, and a tactful expression.

"Already finish."

"It's not even ten yet."

"Finish nine-fifteen. You are American."

"Yes."

"We don't finish late like America. Here—" He slapped his hands together as if trying to knock dust off them. "Everyone home by ten. Music curfew. You want some drink? If not, I close."

"I'll have a vodka," I said. "I guess you must know Rzupinski."

He said hesitantly, "Very well."

"Does he still play here sometimes?"

"Not so often."

"He lives in Warsaw?"

He blinked. "Of course."

The vodka was like a bonfire of silk.

I said, "I'm interested in making a recording while I'm here. I play the clarinet."

"Yes."

"There is still a good recording studio in Warsaw?"

This was vodka taking a whip to my better self.

He gave a deep sigh. "I don't know. Everything a big mess everywhere. But you make recording here if you like. Stanko makes two recordings here. Makowicz also. You know? And many others. If you like—if you pay—why not? We do it in the daytime."

"I need to find a good rhythm section. Perhaps you can recommend some people. Bass, drums, piano."

He nodded. "I will give telephone numbers. Maybe they speak not good English, I am speaking not good, but you have Polish friend, yes? How long you stay?"

"I'm not sure. I'll go to Cracow for a couple of days after Christmas, then I come back. Maybe we can make the recording afterwards. Do you know an engineer?"

"I can find."

"What do you think all this will cost me?"

He thought very hard. He said, "One afternoon, I will ask from you—" He nodded and kept nodding. "Fifty dollars. The engineer will ask from you same, with tape. Musicians maybe less, maybe same."

"For how many hours?"

"Hours, doesn't matter. One hours, six hours, how long it takes. I have music start at night seven-thirty, you must finish before."

Two hundred fifty dollars to make a recording with full rhythm section—even if the whiff of hard currency had raised the price, it still wasn't much. At that moment, between the snow and the vodka, I felt exposed to the bone; I hadn't realized how desperately I wanted to achieve something while I was stuck here.

I said, "I heard an old record of Rzupinski. With a very strong rhythm section. Perhaps you know who I mean. Will you find them for me? Will you telephone? Or if not them, the strongest players you know."

He blinked. "If you want, I can find. When?"

"The thirtieth?"

I wrote it on a napkin to be sure.

"What time you start? You can leave me fifty dollars now? And you telephone?"

"Let's start at eleven, on the thirtieth," I said.

I had U.S. cash in my pocket.

He said, "Why not?"

_____ (Amsterdam)

I n September I visited Holland again, a self-propelled trip—no London gig, solid work back home passed on to friends. Six weeks of Maja's letters and telephone calls after my last visit, even a postcard from Benjamin, had convinced me I belonged back with them on the other side of the Atlantic.

I put out the word that I was looking for someone to sublet my Manhattan apartment; I began to turn down January gigs. I'd saved a small cushion, enough for six months in Amsterdam until the ball got rolling again. I was determined, though, to spend part of it on a recording session of my own music that I'd put off for far too long.

This was as much my agent Barney Klinger's idea as mine. When I explained my plans in his office—decorated only with his own paintings, which inexplicably were always of volcanoes erupting—he shook his head and said, "Cheez, Europe, I don't know," as if he hadn't been booking me there regularly for four years now. "Do us both a billygoat favor," he added in his demure way, "and make the recording first. Why can't I find anything around here?" he yelled to his wife, who functioned as his typist and occasionally baked unpronounceable old-world pastries for me. "Give me something real unique I can take to a record producer, buddy. Say, you interested in a cruise at the New Year? Let me know Friday—no, I won't be here Friday. Be sure to give me a solid date when you're leaving. Sako says we put together the right set-up, he'll offer three weeks in Tokyo next summer. Maybe he wants a harmonica and a whoopee cushion in the group, do I know how that billygoat thinks? Cheez."

As a gift for Benjamin I dug out a revered souvenir of my own childhood: a 3–D panel from 1967 or '68, a cinema lobby gift from my aunt and uncle when they'd taken me to see *2001: A Space Odyssey* at the height of my own galactic phase. The 3–D still worked—I suppose 3–D never breaks—it showed a scene from the film, the space station revolving like a great mother with seedling ships and pods floating off among the stars.

He welcomed it and me with excitement. No unmanly hugs, but a sense of momentous event that I was back, that there would soon be special trips to the movies, perhaps without the ball-and-chain of his mother; that we'd go out for pizza sometimes; that I'd become a familiar presence in the flat, with my clarinet, and speculations on the ongoing interstellar war between the Robot Hordes and the deadly Groosshh. I sensed his pleasure at having, once again, a male ally, and perhaps a contentment that someone had come a long way to visit him, if only for ten days.

In July I'd seen Amsterdam as a city built to human proportions, that one could become fond of easily. Now I recognized I could make my own way of life here and be happier than in New York. The only aspect of New York I enjoyed now, apart from work, was leaving the place, even for only a weekend gig upstate.

Maja suggested I start taking Benjamin to school, as Simon once had. "If you're going to live with us," she said, "this can be your job." Wonderful, I thought. I thrived on routine; I'd accompany him each morning. On the way home I'd find a favorite, as yet undiscovered café, read the *Herald Tribune*, and be back at our also as yet undiscovered flat by ten for three hours' serious clarinet. I imagined, naturally, that Maja would have a job by then and I'd have the daily privacy to practice seriously.

I couldn't help but wonder how much she missed Simon, though she seemed to have ascribed him to the past; if they were still in touch I never found out. We couldn't avoid the sensation that both our lives were in abeyance until I arrived there for good. When I suggested that she begin looking for a larger flat for us, she said, "I don't want to try to describe some place to you on the telephone and then it's not what you want when you arrive. You can surprise me with something after we get back from Poland. No houseboats and no cellars, that's all. And no other Polacks for neighbors."

Usually Maja bicycled Benjamin to school, with him perched behind her. I wasn't prepared to risk this myself. On my second morning we took him—a rehearsal—via two trams. I was surprised by the pristine school courtyard full of slender Dutch mothers, all wearing leggings, poised by bicycles, like some new race of tall shapely women saying good-bye to their energetic children then pedaling off alongside the canals of upright houses.

On our first adventure without his mother Benjamin and I made a serious error. At the tram transfer we rattled off on the right tram in the wrong direction. My fault: this cost us fifteen minutes. Once correctly school-bound, crossing canal after canal, I couldn't remember where to get off for the ten-minute walk, and neither could Benjamin. Trusting to instinct, we got off much too soon and had a complicated, far lengthier trek. The boy was now thoroughly enjoying our being lost, thinking it might gain him an hour off from school and a certain prestige when he finally arrived.

"We don't come this way, usually," he said, with grave understatement. We were walking along hand in hand, I trying to press the pace—every side street in Amsterdam looks identical to a newcomer. He started to hum and sing in English, the theme song from the *Daniel Boone* television show of my youth. He had it well memorized and it annoyed me slightly that, stashed away somewhere in the attic of my brain, I too still kept all the words.

We finally located the school, Benjamin ran in, and eventually I found my way back to the flat. That evening I realized where he was getting his outdated Americana. While the Dutch TV channels showed only a few quality English-language programs, with Dutch subtitles, for their half day of broadcasting, a new channel beamed from Britain across the continent showed hour after hour of the junky U.S. series of the fifties and sixties, paced with bursts of moronic pop music between. Benjamin plonked himself contentedly in front of the TV set when his homework was done, and sat unmoving before America's detectives, hillbillies, shipwrecks, fugitives, and magicians until bedtime.

When I remarked that he was committing them to memory, Maja said, "Are you an expert in bringing up a child?"

"No, but I can see how bad these programs are."

"They're a good way for him to learn English. He's just nine and he speaks and reads three languages. How many do you speak?"

"One and a half."

"You watched them when you were his age, yes?"

"A bit. I read a lot of the time. Or practiced."

"So," she said, "find Benjamin an instrument and start him on some lessons. Or let him try yours."

"It's not an instrument for a beginner. I'll find him one."

"You know I can't afford to buy him both an instrument and a teacher," she said. "When are you moving over here, anyway?"

It was the same question Benjamin asked me one evening. I'd gotten into the habit of tucking him into bed before Maja came in to kiss him good night. The game was to leave our saga of interplanetary warfare at some cliff-hanger ending for him to dream about, like an old-style serial. I would delicately help him hide a spaceship or robot under his pillow so his mother wouldn't suspect it might go into action the instant the lights were out and his door half shut.

This particular night he said, "You're coming back, aren't you?"

"Of course I am. As soon as I can arrange things in New York."

"That won't take very long," he said seriously, man-to-man.

"I don't think so, either."

Usually I shook hands with him rather formally—it was his idea, our private joke of a Daniel Boone good night. This time without thinking I bent to kiss his forehead, and felt his arms hurriedly clasp and unclasp my neck before he turned his face to the pillow, embarrassed.

How could I not come back? I thought. I'd be crazy not to move here.

Maja and I disagreed, though, about money. She wanted everything split down the middle because she didn't want to feel she owed me anything. But when I said, "Couldn't we get a much larger flat if you worked?" she insisted that she couldn't take any serious steady job and legally remain on her barely adequate government payroll. In three months' time, she said, perhaps six, that situation would be more stable and she could get proper employment, perhaps back in the television studio. Meanwhile there were a few interesting photography courses coming up. "Why should I become a waitress for three months?" she said. "I did this when I was eighteen. Or do you want me to go with Saskia back to the peep show?"

"Of course not."

"If you want a lot of other men looking at me," she said in bed one night, her mouth at my ear, "I don't mind. Or do you mind? Do you, hmm?"

It was thrilling to make love quietly, to avoid waking the boy. Maja and I slept on a futon that unrolled in the living room. In a way I knew I hadn't earned yet, I felt myself becoming rooted, not simply as Maja's lover but as the man in a family. I found it made me want her even more. On cool September nights neither of us went to bed nude—she wore a black silk negligee I'd brought her. By virtue of being inches too short, it made her look rapacious. Poised above me, made as pale as a photographic negative by a streetlamp and the frugal Dutch moon opening a shutter in rainclouds, she would pause, rear back, slide the black silk off her shoulder and then fall forward, her hair tumbling across my forehead, her breasts dragged across my mouth.

She spent her days as if they were pocket change, in a daily round of a few duties to Benjamin, an hour or two at a gymnasium to keep herself in shape, perhaps a photography class or at a café with friends, but generally in a kind of active idleness that lacked the impetus to make tomorrow any different from today. Her head was full of plans for travels, photographic expeditions once she acquired proficiency, journeys we might make together, even accompanying me on tour—the theme of South America recurring like a nostalgic tango. Sometimes she joked about being employed to carry the clarinet case and keep my instrument polished.

There were other games, like seeing how much noise she could get me to make when Benjamin was away at school; I learned the pleasures of losing. Other times she seemed to enjoy saying no.

She would say, "Why? Because it keeps up my appetite. Yours for me also." And how could I object, since she could surprise me in the shower on the morning of my return to New York—my eyes closed, my mind on the soap, startle me with two hands stealing around, a long body slithering against mine as I turned, then seeing the water stream across her as she sank down, coddling me swiftly and hungrily into her mouth, until my morning coffee boiled over?

On Christmas Eve in Warsaw, night actually fell around noon. It was, Maja said, a dark miracle.

Late that night Lena told us that, in fact, the Virgin Mary had been seen by a young girl at a hamlet in the countryside shortly before lunch. She'd gone to fetch her brother and there stood the Madonna, not more than a hundred feet away, all in black, with an eerie crimson and yellow aura against the snow.

This hadn't been reported on the news. In a country where no one had faith in the telephones, the event was transmitted by the mysterious Polish bush telegraph that echoed like drums through the wilderness. By the end of the year (we later learned) 250,000 people had made pilgrimages in the cold to that very spot in the folded fields by the little girl's hamlet, and the Madonna's visit was blessed, and its meaning argued over and over.

All I knew was that it suddenly got dark early in the day while Maja and I were standing in a queue to buy vodka for her stepfather. I saw Maja cross herself, a new gesture for her as far as I was concerned, and everyone in the line started muttering balefully. Though the city's machinery was in perpetual disorder, Polish queues were usually ordered and uneventful; nobody broke in front, no one pushed, people were polite or made sardonic jokes. Now I saw them worried and a few simply hurried away.

It got darker.

"More snow," I said hopefully.

"Snow is finished," said Maja. "This is not a good sign, on Christmas. People are very superstitious here."

An hour later we were in another, seated queue—on hard concrete stairs outside a doctor's office. Maja had insisted there would be fewer patients because of the holiday. Ever frugal, she saved up her ailments for her return here every year. This time it was occasional sharp pain in her lower back. The waiting room had a few wobbly chairs and lackluster magazines. No one spoke.

The doctor was an overworked woman who might've been in her early forties and looked a decade older. She nodded wearily to Maja, who didn't belong in that company of the coughing and gray-veined. When Maja returned five minutes later she said bitterly, "I do this every year. I should know better. They write prescriptions for drugs they know they don't have in the pharmacies. If I buy here on the black market it's the same money as if I buy in Amsterdam. Except the drugs are no longer good. I waste my time."

"What did she prescribe?"

Maja glanced at her fellow patients to see if any understood our conversation. She said under her breath, "What do you expect? What they prescribe for everything in this country. Painkiller."

That evening I met Maja's mother for the first time. She was Maja's antithesis: a short dumpling of a woman, with the same eyes but little grace or beauty in her face, only an impassive patience. I couldn't reconcile her with the statuesque mother I'd imagined meeting for months; I had difficulty seeing Maja eventually come to resemble a woman with apparently no lightning in her. She was extremely courteous, with an air of great occasion that I thought must have more to do with her daughter's presence than the holiday.

She ushered us in, wiping her fingers on a smudged apron. The flat was spartan, spotless, and suffocatingly hot. Benjamin was playing in front of a mantle (no fireplace) in a T-shirt, sending the American robots I'd given him across a brown and yellow rug in gladiatorial sallies. A few small framed reproductions of Rembrandt and Van Gogh were fading along with the wallpaper; carved rural knick-knacks stood arrayed on the mantle.

From his corner armchair, his feet up, Maja's burly stepfather Bruno greeted us enthusiastically. A vodka glass was glued to his hand but he received a bottle of Zubrowska with profound delight, as if he hadn't seen one of these faithful soldiers in years. He clapped a hand firmly on my shoulder, vised it in welcome, and announced in Polish that he and I were going to drink until morning.

"No, you're not," said Maja. "He's an American."

I didn't care what she had to say to save me, I was only grateful. She might as easily have explained that the next morning I would be leaving for Cracow without her.

The meal was many courses—I counted an even dozen, keeping track in order to pace myself against the expansive, bushy-haired champion on my left. There was no meat, but a series of vegetables in brothy sauces, potatoes, a borscht, dumplings, and something like gefilte fish, followed by little seedy cakes.

We got quickly past the translate-for-the-foreigner stage and I simply had to look happily hungry. I spoke mainly with Benjamin, who was clearly the master of the household. Bruno and I wound up drunk with him on the rug a couple of hours later, playing galactic combat, each laughing uproariously at remarks by the other which neither understood, making spaceship noises and fending off Benjamin's requests to let him try a glass of vodka. He must've sensed we were having even more fun than he was, though I was almost ready to roll around on the carpet like a dog.

At a timely point in the evening, coffee rescued me. Presents would soon be opened, and Benjamin packed off to bed, most of his gifts having been granted several days earlier. Bruno sat beside me on the sofa speaking very softly and slowly, like a patriarch bestowing an admonition. He must've been in his late sixties, a few years older than Maja's mother, but he looked much younger and indestructible, with that sense not of good health but sheer toughness which comes to people who have worked physically very hard all their lives. What was this wall of a man saying to me in such a measured, cherishing voice?

"He is telling you," said Maja, "all about the war. What happened to him during the war. His house, his family, how he fought the Germans. He wants you to look at his hands. He says those hands rebuilt Warsaw."

"Is he telling the truth?"

"He was a builder, yes."

Now he was up and rummaging in a drawer. He came back with three threadbare medals. I thought he was going to put them on, then I thought he might weep; Maja's mother said something and he exhaled an enormous whistling sigh. He wiped his nose, poured us both the last dregs of the vodka, downed it in a hero's gulp and forced me to do the same. Then I, too, felt ready to weep.

Benjamin had changed into his pajamas and came back to wish us good night. Bruno ushered him over and with great ceremony pinned the three medals on the boy's pajamas jacket, ruffled his gleaming hair, and gave his backside a good wallop. Then he picked him up under one arm and carried him down the hall, Benjamin cheerfully protesting all the way.

I don't recall what Maja brought her mother from Amsterdam. I had Belgian chocolates and a green cardigan for her, and a prize bottle of Johnny Walker for Bruno, which I suggested they keep under lock and key until morning. My remark got translated and I had a success. Their present to me had cost them a week's salary: a souvenir book of Warsaw, black-and-white photographs with text in English.

When I thanked them they looked uncomfortable—not because I didn't seem pleased, for I was very touched—but because they knew I knew how little choice they'd had in what to buy.

What I carried around with me, the troublesome aura of the foreigner, was alternatives. This was the gift I could not bring to them, and that they knew they could not receive. So it was just as well I'd brought whiskey instead.

_____(NEW YORK)

That was a bleak period in New York, October and November: not accepting gigs too far in advance, trying to take advantage of what seemed like a last chance to record my own compositions with friends and a studio engineer who owed me many favors, and trying to placate Maja over the telephone.

She didn't seem to understand that I couldn't clear out of my flat, secure all my professional connections, and be ready to move transatlantic, all in a few days. Nor could she understand why my recording couldn't be done by Monday morning, why I'd let other people's schedules delay me for weeks and weeks.

My recording sessions, scattered aimlessly over that period, were lackluster at best: I should've realized that I could not commit worthwhile performances to tape while packing up six years of my life and haggling with a landlord. My friends played well, I sounded half asleep and out of practice; the first time I felt I'd played badly, truly badly, in years. I squandered both my friends' musicianship and the free studio time due me from that engineer.

"You should wait until you get to Europe to record," Maja argued over the phone one afternoon, when I tried to convey that such an opportunity wouldn't come my way again anytime soon, and shouldn't be put off or wasted. "Everything will change for you as soon as you arrive. Then it might be more interesting, you know."

"This is my last gasp of New York," I said. "That should be interesting enough."

But it wasn't.

Another letter. She sent it six weeks before I left New York for good. I was too frenetic, trying to organize those invaluable recording sessions, to see what was written as plainly as anyone could have asked. Just not plainly enough for me.

A'dam, 30 October

Kochany!

It seems without point to try to give you any news, because of the telephone all the time. We should cut this down, it's very expensive and there are other ways to spend the money. Brazil? Buenos Aires?

So there is no news. I am every day at the pool to swim and do yoga. Perhaps they can give me some work ("on the arm" as we say in Polish) ten hours a week that doesn't touch my status with the government.

I should say there is some news. I hear from the Dutches that it will be another six months at least before they find me and Benjamin our flat. When they find it for us it should be large, at least two bedrooms but possibly more. But this means not until spring or summer. You know how small the flat is here and you know (I hope!) how much space your dragon needs. And even if you don't want to think of me as a dragon, you need to think about how much space three people can eat, especially when one is a child who goes everywhere & one has long legs (you remember my legs? or has it been too long?) & the other is a musician who practices all day . . .

I don't say anything more than this. You think of what you want to do. And we don't have to decide now.

You need to remember to get your Polish visa before you leave the U.S. Because I hear they are a little bit difficult for the Christmas holidays. I don't think there is a problem if you ask in New York. Not here. Be sure you don't wait too late to start, Polacks love to make things problematic if they can.

Remember to bring me some surprises from New York.

The other news is that I think you should try to come as quickly as possible. Because it's taking too long and seriously, I am an impatient woman. If it's too difficult to organize your recording then forget it, do it later, but come here as soon as you can. You should imagine that there are ten, twenty, fifty handsome young men asking me to drinks, every night, to dinner and more, & must I turn them all down?

I am sure you are in the same situation in New York. So I think you'd better hurry over, if this is what you want, and we decide everything else afterwards.

I thought on you all morning.

Benjamin sends you a big hug. Me too.

Your M. (for now!)

P.S. I saw in a book of Japanese haiku a title that would be good for when you do a recording:

THE SONG OF THE NARROW FLUTE

I like this very much. I think you should use it.

I remember reading that letter, feeling the bite of ultimatum, dismissing it, rereading it several more times; there were a few tense telephone calls that left me tenser. Yet, having persuaded her to leave Simon, I still didn't consider that she could far more easily leave me.

The fifty other men didn't really matter to her, nor even the one or two who doubtless actually came and went before I boarded my transatlantic flight in December. By that time I was no longer to be won, I was only to be waited for, and she preferred it the other way around. With me keeping her waiting, she must've been face to face with the void at the center of her days.

I can rationalize now that love—not the deep affection of two people for each other, but the mysterious radioactive desire that ticks away in its shielded underground sanctuary—has a half-life that cannot be tampered with, nor accurately known until it is too late. Because when all the radioactivity has been safely put to sleep and love has lost its risk, its ticking, why bother? With Maja and me, our half-life of time apart turned out to be only a few months: I calculated wrong.

I was still too young to taste on my own tongue how aggressively she felt time leaving her, slipping away like a dwindling family fortune. That August she'd turned thirty-three: should invaluable years of allure and power be wasted waiting for another slow musician to organize his career and come join her? ("Musicians notice every sound around them. Except the voice that's telling what they must hear the most," she said once, speaking of Rzupinski.) After all, what had she left Poland with, going into her own desperate, voluntary exile? A son and a single suitcase: I could not be taken seriously.

All a matter of timing. No one should've understood better than a musician.

—As if it might have been any different between us had I gone over there two months earlier.

This is as forgiving as I can make it.

_____ (C R A C O W)

Alone in Cracow, I saw her everywhere. In the long-limbed schoolgirls strolling brazenly, insolently around the medieval square on a rare sunstruck morning. In the more urgent walk of young women, many of them as striking as she, promenading with the occupied air of belonging to someone else and the dazzle of taunting angels. I saw echoes of Maja in all of them, as if I were unwittingly trailing not her but her shadow other, her secret double, through the fogs and mist drifting about the old townhouses, through the intermittent snowfalls.

Wojciech and his two boys took me around Cracow over the next few days. It was no relief to be away from Warsaw, for Maja still suffused and suffocated me. I felt haunted by her, hunted by the realization of what the last couple of weeks added up to, most of all wracked by the realization I could've been so wrong. My own internal vision was laughable, and that I was here and she was there seemed final. A giant, murderous asteroid was hurtling down upon the very spot where I stood, and it was too late to leap out of the way.

I didn't call her, much as I wanted to: I knew it would do me no good. I rejected the idea of flying over to Amsterdam a few days before she did, and decamping entirely from Doctor Otto's before she returned. Though I couldn't quite hold out hope, I didn't yet accept as fact that I could've come all this way to wind up alone.

At the end of even a minor tragedy the hapless hero still thinks there is a dramatic gesture which can save him, if he can just find it. Only too late does he realize, with astringent clarity, that the machinery is far more complex, and all was set in motion against him long before he ever noticed anything amiss.

With Wojciech and his boys I strolled alongside the winding river, I saw the old university of Copernicus, I visited the enormous castle and its church where most of Poland's kings and queens and poets lie in subterranean vaults, defying century after century of invaders. We climbed innumerable stairs to the belfry and like the boys I rapped superstitiously on that massive medieval bell; I made my wish for all to be as it had been with Maja months ago while looking out over the misted city swaying like a detailed scale model below me. And wondering how many other frustrated lovers had stood like imbeciles on this very spot and asked for the same favor.

I was surprised, down below, when Wojciech spoke of one of those entombed poets as even greater than he. How admiringly his two boys gazed at him, knowing he was making a joke, listening for a deeper fatherly truth in what he was saying as he walked, holding their mittened hands.

I saw why Vera annoyed Maja so: the one who'd stayed

behind was better off than the one who'd left. Vera was solemn, determined, and regal with her pale skin and raven hair. She was also a very relaxed person who had, in Polish terms, defiantly succeeded. She seemed absolutely sure of herself, and content bringing up the two boys despite the peculiar circumstances with Wojciech. She said she had a contract to write her autobiography and was planning to speak frankly about all her lovers: the resultant best-seller would pay for her sons' university in the West. Wojciech seemed still in love with her, but clearly they'd arrived at a truce that worked.

And Vera made me feel welcome. She assured me I could practice as much as I liked, not to worry, it was good for the boys to hear me play and to shut the door of my little bedroom wasn't necessary. She reluctantly showed me a video clip of one of her performances—the sort of mildly sexy Europop that doesn't make it to the States. I complimented her and she accepted my remarks with a nice cynicism. This was a good career, and nothing more.

My world narrowed to this self-contained medieval part of Cracow. I never took one of the pale-blue and cream trams to the more recent parts of the city; anything here later than Chopin didn't interest me. I wanted to pretend I wasn't breaking bread with the present. Around the vast square with its skinny old women peddling forlorn apples and flowers, people still erected little nativity crèches, an ancient Christmas tradition, and the best ones went in some museum. It was a kind of victory over the Soviet Army that this was allowed at all.

I saw on my own the Kazimierz, the once-Jewish quarter where presumably my grandfather had lived—I had no address for him, and anyway, what of my grandfather could still be present in that quarter of derelict streets, an odd moldering synagogue here and there? I preferred to imagine him walking the grand square, humming songs to himself at the sight of pretty girls on the way to the conservatory—at which I was unable to look up his name because the place was padlocked shut for the holidays.

So I went to the cafés, to interrupt my obsessive walks, and sipped and watched the other people and tried to read. Maja had told me that no other city in Poland had such a vibrant café life, partly because of the university, mainly because Cracow's nature was to sit and talk.

"Most of the best cafés," she'd said, "are underground ones."

"Forbidden by the authorities, you mean."

"No, in the cellars."

These were the cafés right around the university, whose cakelike buildings looked as edible as the rest of old Cracow. Downstairs I found catacombs with students smoking furiously, drinking creamy coffee, and munching lavish pastries while they studied, argued, and brooded. Few spoke English; I was treated with suspicion. They may have admired Reagan, and dreamed of emigrating to the States, but an American saying hello made them nervous.

At every turn I was frustrated, and I kept asking myself if this was all Poland added up to, these people going round in their maddening closed circles like wary wrestlers. I couldn't pretend it had nothing to do with me; but for an accident of history I'd have been one of them. Surely this was why I'd gone after Maja in the first place, pulled by that part of myself in her—even now, I still felt pulled mightily. Yet I couldn't savor any special connection with people here, any secret homecoming. I only wanted to leave, even if I didn't have anywhere to go. In that sense I was truly Polish, since half of them didn't feel they belonged here either.

One streetside café drew me every day—Wojciech had

taken me there my first morning. Because of an unpronounceable name I called it the Café Marzipan, full of gnarled marionettes, and sketches and paintings of the artists and writers and musicians of the city from the years just before the First World War. Here, I thought, my grandfather must've sought solace from the fog and snow much as I did, in the dark back salon with its amber lamps turned low, and its stiff armchairs like wooden thrones, and the gorgeous waitresses who never consented, perhaps only because I never asked, to let me take them home and untie their apronlike frocks. In this serene sanctuary I passed hour upon hour, trying to read, trying to settle Maja and that sadness which is like acute pain in the mind. And trying to prop myself up for this Warsaw recording I'd committed myself to but seriously doubted I could bring off: I sensed a final Polish failure looming.

Only in the warm arms of this café, surrounded by mementos of talents of the past—talents emigrated or killed off by the Nazis or crushed by the Soviets—could I feel any possibility in Poland, any sense that another generation of the people who'd made the palace in the Warsaw park must surely exist. It was an outsider's view, I know, but that vision of a country waiting, ever waiting to be restored to itself, penetrated deeply.

It was challenged by a sense of futility when, after every few coffees, I'd get up to go to the men's room in the Café Marzipan's tiled hallway. A fretful woman sat with her little money dish and beside it, a few meager scraps of toilet paper—several bowel movements' ration laid out—waiting for you to admit your more serious need to her at an admission price of two cents per wipe.

Nothing I thought in those days stayed with me for very long: the act of thinking it, or feeling it, doomed it. I imagined myself on an endless succession of trains, always shuttling load after load of heavy bags and musical equipment, continually late, missing a connection and arduously trying to shift all those belongings from one windy platform up steep hard stairs to the next, never able to carry them all myself, moving my life in segments, not knowing where I was going. Was the edge of despair being unable to imagine what might come next? Perhaps nothing would come next. I thought: I have arrived in Poland at last.

I was practicing long hours, if halfheartedly; I knew it was a terrible idea to try making a recording at this moment, especially with players I didn't even know. The last thing I needed was a second musical disaster this winter after what'd happened in New York. I thought: I'll leave Poland for good the day before the New Year. Let the guy at the jazz club keep the fifty bucks, it doesn't matter. I won't be back here ever, I'll call him and cancel, no explanations are necessary.

But the airline offices were closed, and Wojciech decided to stay a few days longer. So in the end I arranged a train ticket for the evening of the twenty-ninth, back to Warsaw.

Maja telephoned once, when I was out. Vera spoke to her. She left no message other than to ask how I was, and I didn't call back, since I didn't really want to provide the answer.

On my final day in Cracow, in the gloom of early afternoon—the old city captured by harpies of mist and under the threat of more snow—I found my way back one last time to the Café Marzipan. That was when I saw my grandfather. At least at that moment and for hours after, I was sure it was he.

He was sitting in an opposite nook of the café, an elderly gent with a full head of wavy white hair, an austere face, and restless eyes. He wore a familiar blue suit but no spectacles—so his sight had improved. He was sipping a glass of wine, and I could glimpse him only when he leaned forward out of the recesses of his armchair so that the dim lamplight fell on his face. Then he would replace the wine glass on the tablecloth with his long fingers, lean back, and recede into the shadows again.

I noticed that the attentive, usually adoring waitresses didn't pay him any attention, but no matter how much wine he sipped, his glass was always half full. His fingers tapped nervously on the fluted stem, as if he were keeping time with a private melody. So this is what you're here for? I thought. To remind me what I should be listening to? I get it, I understand, you won't have to remind me again.

Shaken, I tried to go back to my book. When I looked up again a young lady with glossy brown hair had joined him, her back to me—she was perched forward in her armchair, doting—I knew that if she turned she would be beautiful.

I paid my bill hastily: I did not want the illusion shattered. As I stood up to go, he leaned forward to take his wine glass one last time, and lifted it toward me in a respectful grandfatherly farewell. At that moment I chose to see it also as luck, tendered from one musician to another.

_____ (AMSTERDAM)

I left New York for good on a witheringly cold day in mid-December—two months, according to Maja, behind schedule.

I'd given up my lease in return for "evacuation money"—no changing my mind now. My belongings were sent to my parents in Boston. They expressed parental misgivings about my leaving the country for a woman (and one with a child) whom they'd never even met; I assured them that I had no intention of marrying anytime soon. For all their worries they understood that a significant career might be made overseas, and I know it cheered my mother to think I'd be only a ferry away from her family in London. She'd come to the States on account of my father, so they could both understand my giving Europe and Maja a try. If they realized how obsessed I was, they concealed it.

Dutch customs officers are discreet: they waved through the American in jacket and tie who was obviously moving

to Amsterdam, and painstakingly searched the potential ter-
rorists. I came out of immigration wheeling two carts of my
suitcased belongings—clothes, sheet music, cassettes, books.
Dehydrated and groggy from a month's exhaustion and a
difficult morning changing planes in Brussels. Surprised at
the morning stillness in A'dam after last night's icy wind in
New York. I kept thinking: ten months after Port Stilton . . .

Maja met me outside the terminal, where I stood blinking
in a nipping and eager air, beneath a lower sky than I'd
left the day before. She was in tights, a hip-hugging sweater,
low boots and a leather bomber jacket. Her hair longer, at
her shoulders now.

My relief at finally arriving, at seeing her, was over-
whelming: all my weariness and worries slid away.

She raised her eyebrows at my two carts of luggage, stuck
her tongue out at me, and bestowed a chaste kiss on my
lips.

She said, "Don't you think you brought too much?"

I laughed and hugged her. "I'm not sure I brought
enough."

She said, "You know, for weeks now I wasn't sure you
were really coming."

"It isn't real to me yet, either."

We were trundling my luggage carts along the terminal
sidewalk.

She said, "After you telephoned from Brussels this morning, I realized that I don't love you anymore."

"Now you tell me."

She said, "I'm serious."

I tasted bile coming up, and swallowed. "Can't we talk
about this later? I'm very tired."

Small talk in the taxi; small talk over coffee in the borrowed flat when my bags were finally lugged up two flights
of stairs; small talk before she left on her bicycle to fetch

Benjamin from school. I tried to put myself in her position. How nervous would I have been if she'd suddenly joined me for good in New York? After so many months of talk and preparation? The idea of my moving in must've seemed different when I was still thousands of miles away. Now that I was actually here, and she was confronted with me and my baggage, I needed to find the best way to put her at her ease.

Surely all we needed to find ourselves again was to make love.

I was a good musician, but I still didn't know how to listen. I was asleep when they came home from school. I got up for dinner and presented Benjamin with a book on dinosaurs to distract him from the American television of twenty years ago. With luck it would keep him sated until Christmas. Apparently excited at the prospect of my living with them, eventually he was pushed off to bed.

Maja got right to the point. A much longer time apart had been "wasted" than she'd anticipated; she knew she still cared for me; she thought she was still attracted to me.

"But I'm not sure I want to share a place with you," she said. "I'm not right now in love with you. Perhaps I will be, again, but it was too much time. You can stay here as long as you want, maybe in a week I am used to you again and I realize how much I love you. I don't know. Maybe you want to find a place of your own and we see what happens that way. Maybe you want to go back. So it's up to you."

"Why didn't you tell me before? I don't have anywhere to go back to now."

"I didn't realize until this morning. When I went to meet you at the airport. I think I didn't really believe you would come. After all your excuses for months about not being ready for Amsterdam."

"They weren't excuses. You know I came here for you. Not for the damned canals."

"Not for your music also? To put your career moving in a much better direction? And not for Benjamin, too?"

I thought hastily, stopping myself on the verge of explosion: Calm down, cool it, you won't settle anything right now. Accusation will only drive her off.

She said, "Anyway, you will decide what you decide. You know you can stay here as long as you want to. Maybe I'll change my mind tomorrow, I can't say. If I thought of this clearly before I would tell you before. And already I feel much better to see you sitting here. You know it took me a long time to get free of Simon, maybe it's only that I'm worried about entering the situation again."

"So what do we do about Poland? And Benjamin's holiday?"

"That's up to you." Her tone softened. "It depends what you want. I have three reservations. For Friday. Maybe you don't want to come any longer. But I'd like you to come."

I quickly tried to weigh my apparent choices—to hang around here doing nothing for two weeks while she was away and hope she had a change of heart? Or go with her as we'd planned for months, persuade her gently, seduce her again, while she showed me her country?

Maybe I was crazy to be considering either choice. Perhaps if I said: Forget it, I'll find myself a flat before you get back and don't bother to call when you do—she'd return all honey and fire and open arms.

If I stayed here, though, there was the certain insult of refusing to see her homeland.

And an insult to myself. For years Poland had meant the whole idea of my grandfather to me; now the idea of being so close and refusing to go seemed unnatural. I had no interest in looking for the little village where my ancestors might or might not have lived six generations back. People who went on quests like this always struck me as slightly bogus, and naive in their hope—rummaging around in an empty attic for family heirlooms. But I thought of maybe locating Dilko, of at the very least finding my grandfather's conservatory, and of even saying aloud on medieval streets he'd once walked: At least one of us was able to make a life in music.

I'd thought all along that Simon had made a crucial mistake, never to have visited Poland with her—for it was, surely, where Maja's essential nature came from, no matter how she exiled herself. How could I understand what propelled her if I didn't go? And how could I hope to understand that part of who I was, or at least who my grandfather had been?

I said, "Of course I want to go. I wouldn't miss it. No matter what happens between us."

I even paid for all three plane tickets.

_____ (WARSAW)

It was as an extremely tense musician that I took an afternoon train back to Warsaw, my clarinet case on my knees and what I might record the next day on three contradictory lists across a pad of paper propped on the case. White spotted fields flowed by, a snow leopard's pelt, until we meandered into darkness. I dozed; dreamed of my grandfather encouraging me in the Café Marzipan; woke and wrote down another few possible tunes.

The French were out for the evening, so Maja and Lena were alone in the flat when I arrived, glaring at each other from behind a book and a newspaper. I might never have left as far as Maja was concerned: no change in that weather. She wanted gossip about Vera and Wojciech's troubles and instead got only approval of their arrangement. I was in an aggressive state I knew I had to maintain until I got to the recording session, or else I'd fall to pieces.

Both women insisted, naturally, that no one would show up at the Akwarium Jazz Club tomorrow morning. Lena offered to telephone them for me, and was surprised to hear it was all arranged and that they were worried *I* wasn't going to come.

"I don't know yet if I can be there or not," murmured Maja with trenchant cunning. "I am thinking to take Benjamin to see his father, he lives outside Warsaw."

"Then I guess you can't be there," I said, and took my mug of tea to the back room to practice and go over my tune lists, which now resembled elaborate games of tic-tac-toe.

My musical situation was no clearer in the morning. How do you decide what you're going to play when you're not even sure of the instrumental lineup? I'd spent two hours at Lena's desk, working long after midnight, writing out the chord changes of a dozen tunes I wanted to try and that these players might or might not know, or might not know in the same key.

It was, ominously, the coldest morning I'd yet experienced in Poland. Lena, who was kind enough to set out a delicious breakfast of thick dark bread and a soft white cheese I loved, was muttering about the winter of '78 and citing dire unbelievable statistics of sixty below. The five-minute walk down Marszalkowska past the forbidding Palace of Culture was like winter in a grim fairy tale—frozen clouds obscured the central bulky towers where evil wizards plotted with their henchmen. A tram rattled past packed with standing, wide-eyed people, miserably protected from the old enemy by Soviet engineering. Stunned by the temperature, stamping my boots, I thought: It doesn't matter who's at the club, by the time I arrive I'll be too cold to play, my lips will be frostbitten.

Three men were waiting downstairs at the Akwarium,

vigorously chatting, sipping coffee, unaffected by the weather. One was the skinny manager, relieved to see me. Despite Lena's phone call, the other two must've still doubted the entire proposition. They looked rather wary until we were introduced, then they thawed. Both were in their forties. The bassist, Jerzy, had a clipped beard and a staring expression; his surname seemed familiar. The other was bald, and perspiring in a heavy sweater, he resembled a hired killer, or at least a torturer. He spoke no English; he mimed playing a piano, arms and fingers splayed wide, and laughed sadistically. He had one gold tooth. He said something like, *"Wlrytyz zdn posh ladzyetny?"*

"Tomas," said the manager hurriedly. "Best piano in Warsaw."

Bass and piano alone would sound a little sparse—I'd had my heart set on one of those high energy Eastern Europe blowing sessions where everyone plays as if his freedom depends on it.

"Tomas says, 'What are we going to play?'" said the manager.

"That depends," I began.

At that moment Tomas hummed a few bars of Bernstein in 6/8—the tune that goes

> *I like to live in America*
> *Okay by me in America*

and everyone laughed. I said, "They'll never let me out with the tapes."

Jerzy, the bassist, said, "Drums and guitar are upstairs."

"I don't know if maybe you want guitar also," said the manager. "So I ask him come in. We go upstairs, gentlemen?"

Upstairs a drummer was studiously adjusting his cymbals;

like many jazz drummers, he resembled an accountant. A lanky guitarist in wire-rimmed spectacles, a bit younger than the others, was tuning in a corner and didn't look up.

"My friend Stefan," said the manager, making it clear by his tone that the guitarist was an option, not a necessity. "And this one also is called Jerzy."

He meant the drummer, and I realized with a start that these two—Jerzy & Jerzy—had been the rhythm section on Rzupinski's hurricane recording ten years earlier.

There was another man in the room, his back to me. He wore headphones and was fiddling with the controls on an enormous reel-to-reel that looked nearly antique. A smaller, newer reel-to-reel sat beside it. He turned to be introduced and I saw it was the electronics man who'd changed my dollars at Lena's flat on my first morning. He smiled as if we were cronies as he shook my hand. I thought: I've only been here ten days, and already it's a small country.

He turned back to his equipment. The manager said, "He will make cassette at the same time. And duplication of big tape. If there is trouble with original at the airport, he will send later. You understand? So we can begin when you want."

We tried a couple of tunes to balance the sound levels and to warm up—a slow blues, and a Gershwin standard everyone knew and that I knew I didn't want to play on the recording. I listened back to check the clarinet sound, we made some microphone adjustments, then I took the manager aside and asked if he wouldn't mind suggesting that the guitarist sit out several numbers. I didn't want such a busy rhythm section, I explained, but perhaps he could play on some tunes later in the session. The manager nodded, and spoke in low tones to the guitarist for a moment, who gave a cheerful wave and settled himself by the engineer to listen on a second set of headphones.

It's always like this: an eternity of sound checks and microphone adjustments that make you think you'll never get started. Then once the tape starts rolling the hours are swallowed by the music so afterwards you can't recall the passage of time with any clarity.

I do recall what I told the others before we began, and had the manager translate for me. I said that I'd heard some of them play on recordings, and this made me want to record while I was here. Since I'd never played with them before I didn't want us to try to get anything perfect, I wanted us only to play as hard as possible and as many tunes as possible, as if it were a live performance, without any reluctance. No more than a couple of takes per tune, and we'd sort out what was good and what was not later.

"What if everything is good?" said Jerzy the drummer, and we all laughed, the nervous laugh that means it's time to get started.

Their playing was authoritative, and full of mature ideas—you can soon tell how smart another player is, and I had three brains working around me that day. The bassist had a large tone (he played also in the Warsaw Symphony Orchestra); the drummer was modern in his time, very active and free; the pianist had that precise and shocking harmonic sense for substitutions that seems to come only from players with a background in classical music.

We did two versions of "All the Things You Are," the first a bit hurried, the second clearer in mood, and then we got derailed. I'd suggested we do "Love for Sale" fairly uptempo. I blew a fleet and rather glib solo that dismayed me even as I pulled it off. The pianist said something in a threatening undertone and the manager hurried over and conferred for a moment.

"Tomas says he think—" He paused. "He think maybe you don't sound like this is really what you want to play today." He looked ill at ease with his translation. Tomas spoke again, at length. "He says you are in mood inside yourself, then you must play mood inside yourself, see what happen."

"All right." For days I'd been complaining to myself that no one in Poland listened to what you said; these three men heard more than I did of what I meant. I asked, "Anyone know 'Blue in Green'?"

"B flat," said Tomas, and the two Jerzys nodded.

We played it slowly, ravishingly, for twelve minutes—the piano's solo was almost orchestral in its textures, and he and I took the tune out together in a long jagged counterpoint that neither of us had reckoned on. It would end up being the centerpiece of the record. At the time I heard only severe introspection, an inner inspection, in my playing, but I also felt no barriers; what came out at that moment was what I truthfully felt on that day. Later I would hear what a deep place in myself I was playing from, in a far country among friendly strangers—playing, at least on one cold intense morning, with a lyrical grip and beauty, and acknowledging many questions.

Sometimes it takes only a single tune to put you in the proper pocket for the entire session. We had found our sympathetic material, and we went from ballad to ballad. We did "My One and Only Love," and "In a Sentimental Mood," and a stark "Round Midnight"; we did a fast "Joy Spring" and a slow, intense bossa nova, "How Insensitive," which the guitarist joined in on, and even a delicate "Jitterbug Waltz," the strangest tune Fats Waller ever wrote. I knew there was nearly an hour of music there that might be worth saving. It was after three now, time and energy left for only a couple more tunes.

We'd stopped briefly for coffee and sandwiches earlier, and now we halted for another quick coffee break. At a certain point you feel your energy waning and know, warmed up as you are, that you mustn't give in to the urge to relax. The guitarist, who seemed to have enjoyed himself mostly listening, took his instrument off the stand and before putting it back in the case, strummed idly through a few dense chords from which emerged a snatch of one of my favorite ballads, a graceful Hoagy Carmichael song called "The Nearness of You." My first thought was that I played it much too rarely, even though I often hummed it to myself.

From that thought it took only a moment to get the mikes adjusted for our two instruments. We played two choruses of the tune, I in the most simple way imaginable, concentrating only on tone, playing variations that hugged the melody and wouldn't let it go, while he—what was his name? Stefan?—supported me with those blurred, suggestive chords which a sensitive guitarist can find that sidle in and out of the normal harmony of a song and leave so many unexpected possibilities open for the soloist. The others applauded softly when we were done, the sound engineer gave us the thumbs up, and I thought: Now we can go home.

"One more," said Tomas, with a sinister gleam of his gold tooth. I hadn't realized he spoke any English other than song titles and key signatures. He sat down somberly at the piano and ushered the two Jerzys—the accountant and the professor, I thought of them now—back to their drums and bass. I speak of their appearance only; by this point I was convinced they were one of the strongest rhythm sections on the continent.

"Whatever you like," I said.

" 'Giant Steps.' " His tooth glinted.

I said, "How about 'Moment's Notice'?"

He grunted. It's an equally complicated tune, also by

Coltrane, but more lilting, and more hospitable to the clarinet. Plus I'd played it every night for three months on tour
with Mark and Rob as a way of forcing ourselves to learn,
inch by inch, a chord sequence harrowing to blow inven-
tively on, to really handle melodically, at anything other
than ballad tempo. Besides, I didn't want the two Jerzys
comparing me to the "Giant Steps" they'd done with Rzupinski.

We tore into it, and the generous angel that occasionally
watches over jazz musicians was with me. I was in that ideal
state of knowing the tune inside out without having played
it for several months, so there was a coastal shelf of ideas
built up and waiting to be dredged. I flew through three
choruses, watched Tomas sweat through a careening chorus
of his own that led into one series of eights for guitar, bass,
and drums. We took it out violently, the piano doubling
me on the melody, and ended all together with an almighty
crash. Even Jerzy the Professor gave a grin and looked satisfied.

"Now," said the other Jerzy, "most difficult thing of all.
We try to find taxi."

It was one of the most satisfying hours of my life, listening
to a playback while we took our time dismantling the equipment and putting the instruments away. The four of them
were performing at the club on the third and fourth of
January; they asked me to come sit in and I said of course,
if I was still here.

I paid and thanked them, asked them to give my regards
to Rzupinski should anyone run into him, and we drank
some brandy on the house. When we exchanged addresses
I realized again, a sinking feeling to accompany the brandy,
that I now had no address of my own.

But I had this afternoon on tape.

I'd paid the guitarist, Stefan, as much as the others. He

spoke English fairly well, and I made it clear how pleased I was with our duet, how sorry I was that it hadn't been possible for him to play on more tunes, but the clarinet was easily crowded out. He in turn asked how I'd come to be in Warsaw.

I made a lame remark about having come with a Polish friend and leaving by myself.

He said, "Better than leaving with Polish enemy."

"That's true, I guess."

"From where? From New York?"

"I used to be from New York. Not anymore."

He said, "Look, I give you money back, you must please send me guitar strings." He adjusted his glasses, afraid he was asking too much—a sweet, intellectual guy, I thought, the kind of musician who reads Bergson and Camus in his spare time and tries to take into account the entropy of chaotic matter in his playing. Some jazzers are ardent Go players, others like to bet on the horses.

"I cannot get proper guitar strings here. These are nearly two years old. Is a very big problem for me."

"I don't know when I'll be back in the States, though. If I can find them in Holland I'll send them to you next week."

"Yes, yes," he said, switching into Polish in his excite-ment—his *tak-tak-tak* like a typewriter. Then he peered at me strangely. "Amsterdam?"

"That's where I go from here."

He said, "Who is your Polish friend?"

I told him.

Now it seems a fitting joke, that he and I had played "The Nearness of You" together. But when he spoke I was left speechless for a moment. Should I have been so sur-prised?

He said, "I was Benjamin's father," and removed his spectacles and rubbed his eyes.

That night, with Maja sleeping heavily beside me as the temperature plummeted outside, I had one of those waking dreams that come over you like beating wings when you are prone in darkness and too troubled to sleep.

She and I were in Lazienki Park, by the lake and the palace and those nude statues. It was spring and the trees were vibrant with lilacs. Swans and peacocks patrolled everywhere, couples strolled arm in arm. A kind of overdone spring, the colors so sumptuous I knew I was in a dream even as I walked through it. There was a soundtrack to accompany the technicolor falsity of the scene, a version of music I'd played that afternoon—a slow blues. Maja was recounting with great pride the lovers she'd had, how they surpassed me, and I was nodding agreement, abetting her argument with arcane facts which took her by surprise. I almost seemed to know her in a clinical sense, as if I were her doctor-confessor.

All the while I was thinking: But these are excuses, all these men. Not lovers or friends being remembered, but excuses.

I felt the warmth of the radiant afternoon and decided: I must find an excuse myself.

Then I clapped my hand to my forehead and said to Maja with great consternation, *My darling! I left the kettle boiling on Lena's stove—all that valuable water will be evaporated by now!*

And before she could muster a protest I was away and running. End of the Warsaw Woman Blues, at least as I dreamed them.

When I got up, Maja was finishing her tea and assembling her coat and gloves and scarf and boots to go out.

"I'm taking Benjamin to see his father," she said. "Do you want to come along and meet him?"

I'd told her little of the day before.

"No, thanks."

"He's a wonderful guitarist. I'm sure you'd like him."

"I'm sure I would."

"You can play him the tape you did. He's got a very good critical mind, you know. He has—how do you say? Perfect pitch?"

"I'll stay here, thanks."

"I hope you thought of your costume for the party tonight."

I'd forgotten all about it. "Can't I go as an American jazz musician?"

"Half the Polacks there will be disguised as Americans," she said. "You'd better find something more original than that."

"Maybe I'll go as a cheeseburger."

After she left I told Lena, "You know, I met Stefan yesterday," and explained. I realized, at that moment, that Lena was the only person here I could speak to frankly— perhaps because it was in another language. "Do you think Stefan will tell her?" I asked.

"I hope so. It could be good for her, to be surprised."

"You don't think she's had her share of surprises?"

"I think she prefers to be the one who manufactures them." Lena was regarding me quizzically. "How did you find Stefan?"

"He seemed very sad to be left out of Benjamin's life. I gather he doesn't have a family of his own."

"That's true. But don't forget she was here for a few years and he didn't want to be involved then. He cannot suddenly discover he likes being a father when the boy is already nine."

Stefan hadn't struck me that way, but I had the impression that this was a dissonance left over from Lena's divorce.

She said, "How are you and Maja getting along?"

"Not too well. It looks like we're finished."

I spoke lightly, but heard my voice abruptly on the verge of cracking. I poured myself some tea and stared away from her, two chairs distant at her long dining table.

She said sternly, "Listen to me. She is an old friend but there is something you must understand about her. She is the most selfish person you will ever meet. A person who decides everything. She will not let anyone else make decisions with her because this means she gives up power."

"The selfishness isn't her fault," I said—surprised to find myself vehemently defending her. "It's built into the equation. Who else is there around her but Benjamin? She's just trying to survive."

Lena dismissively swept some bread crumbs before her and away.

"Look, you should have seen what a beauty she was at twenty-two. Not classical but with so much strength she could get anything she wanted. Now she is just beginning to suspect that in a few years she won't have so much strength anymore."

"She's intelligent, she'll be ready."

"Bah! She's stupid. She does nothing, she tries nothing new because she fears she will fail. Or at least have some difficulty at first. And it's written in her law that she must always seem above the success and failure of everyone else. I promise you, if she had come to your recording session she would have made sure it was a catastrophe and convinced you it was entirely your fault."

I said, "I don't believe that. Anyway, I'm willing to support her while she looks for some opportunity, doesn't she realize this?"

"Of course she realizes." Lena laughed mirthlessly. "This is why you scare her."

"I certainly don't scare her. I don't know who does."

"Can't you see? Everything scares her. You come here for ten days, she doesn't pay any attention to you at all, and you do a recording. This drives her crazy. She wants you to be lost here without her. She was complaining about you all day yesterday. The American who has to make an impression wherever he goes."

I wanted her to be lost without me, too—I'd seen myself as rescuing her from Simon, hadn't I? But she wasn't lost at all; she knew how to protect herself far better than I did.

I said, "She knows that kind of impression doesn't interest me."

"I reminded her that you're being a professional. She said, 'You wait, they will be laughing when they hear him play.' Naturally she doesn't believe a single word of this. She says anything to convince herself. Tonight she will find some man or another to make you very jealous." She shook her head. "You should not dream. For you it's dangerous."

I said, "I don't think she understands how much I turned my back on to come to Europe. What I gave up to join her."

"She understands. She told me about every step you took. It proves to her how powerful she still can be. Do you think she would give up her independence so easily? I told you how selfish she is. It will take someone very particular a long time to help her change. Don't let her destroy you because you imagine you are that man."

Her words astonished me: this was Maja's best friend talking. It crossed my mind that maybe she didn't believe a word of what she was saying, it was all spoken out of kindheartedness, to wipe Maja out of my consciousness permanently. Then I noticed the firm set of Lena's brow and jaw as she sat there watching me and I felt a flicker of something else from her, not quite flirtation, but of competition perhaps—for an instant I wanted to grab her, to see what would happen. It was as if we'd both stepped into treacherous waters, and while trying to save me she was feeling their seductive currents swirl around her also.

I covered my eyes for a few seconds—only then realizing I was already in tears. What was I crying for? An illusion, or even a hallucination: the couple that Maja and I had been. How much time had we had? All that feeling from how many days together? A week in Port Stilton, three weeks in New York and three in Amsterdam, ten days here in her frozen country. It was not my country.

What else? We'd been all letters and hope, little more, the ether of in-between. With love one can make sustenance out of very little, for too long, and feed unhealthily until it is too late.

I said shakily, "I know she realizes that she must find serious work. We've talked about it, she's very clear on this. I know she's decided she must move somewhere with her life. Photography, maybe."

Lena said gently, "My dear, do you really think you are the first lover she has made these speeches to?"

_____ (W A R S A W)

O n the last evening of the year we all had
important missions. The French were
in charge of wine and children, Maja and Lena in charge
of costumes. I was in charge of food for the hungry hordes.

Lena was going to the party as a witch, Yves as a buc-
caneer, Anne as Camille. In a felt hat and Lena's trenchcoat
I was either a gangster or a spy, armed with a collapsible
coat hanger in my hip pocket to suggest a gun. Maja was
going as Peter Pan, complete with pert feathered cap, short
green shorts and tights, a flimsy vest, and Benjamin's bow-
and-arrow set, which he'd parted with in return for a promise of chocolate back in Amsterdam. All three children
would be parked at Maja's mother's for the night; Bruno
would have his hands full.

The party was somewhere on the outskirts of Warsaw at
a large gymnasium or public hall of some sort—I imagined
a gargantuan Elks Club for the working masses. Though

theoretically there was no private enterprise in Poland, the party was the brainstorm of a few individuals. There'd be romantic music, the right crowd, as elegant an event as modern Warsaw could muster. It was too late to buy tickets, the three hundred printed were sold out. Neither Lena nor Maja had ever been to this legendary fête, but they claimed that people spoke of it for months afterwards.

By seven the gang had assembled at the flat. Arrangements had been made for the children, costumes assembled, food laid out. Zosia arrived half-undressed as an Arabian dancer, ripe and tipsy. Ulrik too was there, established in his armchair, two private bottles of vodka bulging his jacket pockets. Ulrik was going to the party as Ulrik.

He crooked a finger at me and said, "You want to leave together?"

"To go to the party?"

He waggled his massive head and I realized Andrzej's gorilla comparison wasn't apt. Ulrik was a bull elephant, getting ready to charge, or else stagger to the ground and die.

He said, "To London."

"I'm only going as far as Amsterdam."

"So I let you off at Rembrandt's house." He dismissed mere details as unimportant. "Important thing is, we take ten cases of vodka back through Germany. They see American passport, they don't ask questions. We make a lot of money, we split it. You and me."

"Split it how?"

"Eighty-twenty. My vodka. My car, I do the driving."

"My passport."

He sighed and looked genuinely sorry for himself. "Seventy-thirty."

"Don't you think we'd have a better chance with Benjamin and his mother along also?"

He shuddered. "Less space for vodka."

"How long would it take?"

"Three days. Maybe little less."

"To London?"

"One day to Paris only. One day to sell. Maybe we sell in Amsterdam. One day for problems."

"What problems?"

"Border problems. You have dollars?"

"Some. Not a lot."

He blew smoke from a handmade cigarette that smelled like a mixture of tobacco and border problems. "Dollars are first choice for bribes. We don't have trouble at border crossing, I can tell."

I said the journey sounded like an awful lot of fun to me and I'd think about it all evening. I wondered how much vodka Ulrik could drink in three days, given ten cases to work with. He looked suspicious even telling a joke in an armchair—behind the wheel of an overloaded car he'd be a plea for a thorough interrogation and search. What else was he planning to smuggle? Funny cigarettes? I could just see the East German border guards confiscating my tape.

I left Ulrik gruffly humming an Andrews Sisters tune into his glass. I went to the back room to change, and at this point Zosia, sweeping blithely past me in the hallway, asked me in her very broken English if I thought her veils needed adjusting. I genuinely couldn't tell if she was flirting or only drunk, and for the rest of the evening (was I supposed to have unveiled her and kissed?) she acted insulted and aloof.

In the back room among the otherworldly paintings Maja was standing stark naked—I've never known a woman with her lioness pride about wearing nothing, her conviction that it's how she was meant to be seen. Her costume was laid out on the sleeping bag.

She said, "What were you and Ulrik talking about?"

"Nothing much. Some scheme of his. The usual."

"The usual? Suddenly he's a friend of yours? You should be careful with him. What is it?"

"It's not important."

"It might turn out to be," she said. "You should tell me."

How easily she could be manipulated by her own games, if I put my intentions there.

"Okay, I can imagine," she said. "Whatever it is, you should do it. Good education for a boy scout."

It'd been open warfare between us ever since she returned from taking Benjamin to see his father. To learn that Stefan and I had not only met but played music together, and gotten along, was too much like being insulted or laughed at behind her back. My crime lay in not warning her: she'd felt foolish learning it from him.

I said, "Ulrik's kind of education I don't need, thank you."

"You're such an American," she said quietly. "You think you're not, but you are. You grow up completely in America and everything else is just a mythology. Even your London mother couldn't make you half English. You're always dreaming you'll come back to Europe and find yourself. You're pretending. You all think you'll visit here to find you're a bit Polish but that was two generations ago. None of you deserve to be Polish."

"I promise you, no one in their right mind deserves to be Polish."

"So you should thank Ulrik. Offering to take you away from all of us."

"I don't need his help to leave. I might fly out in a couple of days."

She said confidently, "We'll see what you say after the party tonight. Aren't you worried about what happens when Wojciech comes back from Cracow?"

"You mean worried he might fuck you?"

"Wouldn't you rather it was you instead?" she said.

"Actually, you almost persuaded me about Zosia. Have you seen her costume?"

She stared at me as if she might still make up her enigmatic mind in my favor. Then she said, "Let me get ready. You can dress in two minutes, later on."

It was almost dismaying to be getting somewhere. There was nothing not spiteful to be said, so I went back to helping Yves who, in pirate eyepatch and bandannas and baggy silk trousers, was readying the champagne glasses for the initial celebration here. It wasn't seemly to arrive too soon at this party—ten-thirty, maybe eleven, no earlier. Warsaw too had its strict rules of chic, and when I suggested this to Yves he laughed until I thought he might fall to his knees and weep.

The night was bitterly cold; snow had frozen solid along the roads and Ulrik's car, even packed with seven of us, was drafty. No one knew where the party hall was, precisely. All the approach roads looked the same on a winter night.

We heard a banshee roar like fighter planes homing in for a raid.

"You don't think this is it?" asked Anne.

No one answered her.

Then we saw it: an enormous concrete structure, alive with flashing lights and people wandering around outside as if lost. Someone took our tickets at the door. A front hall had tables laid out, with punch bowls and crackers and cheese and brownies—we soon learned that these were laced with hashish. The party was already a huge mess. A few stairs led to a great hall where hundreds and hundreds of people were dancing in semi-darkness while a strobe light zigzagged across their jumping heads and, on a stage at the back, a band dressed like guerrillas from another planet ground out the hardest, loudest, bitterest, harshest music I have ever heard. To cover your ears made absolutely no difference—it was like being inside a jet engine at takeoff. It was sheer noise, with no music in it whatsoever; hard to believe human beings could make such sounds, and because there was no steady beat to it, the dancing mob all yelled and jumped around wildly, not even together.

"Warsaw chic," yelled Yves faintly in my ear, and began helping himself to food.

Few people were costumed, but most wore some concession to the event, a strange hat or a feather or sunglasses. I'd never seen so many blind-drunk people in one place. They slumped against the walls, or stood shoved together in little clusters of argument, or wobbled around with arms about each other's shoulders.

The women were as drunk as the men. Zosia, who'd helped herself to the brownies, brushed past me twice without even recognizing me. Maja disappeared into the dancing riot, leading Anne and Lena behind her. Yves and I stayed with the food. I never saw Ulrik again.

As I watched the heads rising and falling it struck me how truly desperate these people were—not hungry for food, perhaps, but so starved of something interior that only music which sounded like a re-creation of war could affect them. The pure noise spoke to them and expressed all that the rest of their lives could not in an enormous yell of pain and anger, an obliteration of all subsidiary feeling. It had to be so powerful, because only sheer volume could compensate for the other power that was missing from their everyday lives.

At least I remember trying to think something like this.

A man with straggly brown hair and beard was crawling on his hands and knees out of the mob, as if searching for his contact lenses. He staggered to his feet and pulled himself up the wall to catch his breath; his amazed stare passed over me without registering. Then he closed his eyes, still standing up, put a forefinger to his temple as if it were a pistol, pulled the imaginary trigger, and burst into a paroxysm of helpless laughter.

What was Maja coming back here for? She'd seen the world, she'd gotten away, what drew her back to this place? Was it her family? Was it the need to offer her country to her son? I saw her dancing in the mob, wriggling every which way, making a show of herself even in that melee—what attracted her to such desperation?

At one point for a few freezing moments I wandered outside with Yves, feeling the vodka in my stomach turn to psychological ice; you got drunker simply by standing in the open air. When we went back in he found his way through the mob to dance again with his wife. Even though Anne didn't seem to want to have much to do with him, his strategy was to appear not to care.

Just then Maja came out to the front hall to find me. She was sweating, flushed—she looked like she'd just made love.

"Aren't you coming inside? It's nearly midnight."

"I can hear everything just fine."

"No, we must dance for the New Year." She took my hand, led it around the waist of her Peter Pan getup. She'd lost the little cap.

We stood aside while the man I'd seen on his hands and knees, still arguing with himself, went reeling against a food table and crashed to the floor. Maja watched him with curiosity.

"That's him," she said crisply.

"That's who?"

"The musician you wanted to meet. Rzupinski."

She didn't look back, but pulled me into the noise after

her. Crushed by the heaving bodies, we squirmed around together. I kept thinking how far it was from the Happy Gardens in Port Stilton to the nightmare of this spot, what a long way to come to change the way we danced with each other. There had seemed so much innocence in that little place at the end of the world; no innocence left between us here at all.

At midnight the band roared on without mercy, but a few people with accurate wristwatches let out frenzied yells that were taken up by others and drowned out immediately by the band. So much for the New Year.

A while later we gathered in the front hall, amid the shambles of food and drink. Rzupinski was gone, Zosia lost or unveiled somewhere; and Ulrik, Lena reported, wanted to stay another couple of hours. We'd catch a taxi, there'd surely be taxis out on New Year's Eve, and a taxi would carry five if we paid well.

We began to walk, relieved to turn our backs on the tumult. The night was dense with clouds, but ice gleamed everywhere, illuminating the road. Yves began singing some French air that Lena and Anne took up. There were no taxis. Dizzy with fatigue and vodka, I was revived quickly by the cold. Maja was walking by herself, leading the troops, a few steps ahead of me.

She glanced back and began spinning playfully, coyly. Whirling in her long coat as she walked, talking to herself. By now I was too removed to feel any sadness. I felt only a vague wonder at her apartness and her pride, at how she could carry on capriciously swirling down the road without looking around her and somehow avoid foundering. It was the ones who saw more who wrecked themselves or lost their certainty of vision, and with a pang I thought of Rzupinski.

That was when I had the idea that not to be her lover,

but to be her ex-lover, to be caught in an argument with her, was really the natural state of affairs. To be her present lover, in the grip of a shared passion, was the fluke, and could never last.

Traipsing along in time to my chattering teeth, a wind pushing me down that gray road with the derelict outskirts of Warsaw in silhouette all around, I was suddenly jolted by what made Maja come back here. She would always come back just as, even after her Dutch passport came through, she would keep her Polish passport as well. She'd had chance after chance—and not only Simon—to disconnect herself, to liberate herself from it forever; each time she refused. It wasn't patriotism or family or homesickness, or dissatisfaction with a particular lover, or even a desire to return and show off for old friends. It was out of a deeper need, for this place could be an excuse for not making a life elsewhere. She carried the Polish lack of possibility out of the country with her, and because she wasn't sure what to do with herself, she returned from time to time for another dose to keep going another year.

As I walked behind her and off to the side, I caught her slowing down almost imperceptibly, so that little by little I'd catch up with her. She was humming to herself. We'd walked seemingly for hours—the other three were holding hands, lurching along speaking or singing in French behind us. There were no cars at all on these cold straight roads that ran nowhere. The entire country was at a standstill; only we were moving, like ants interminably trying to find our way home on a path through rubble and ice.

I was almost alongside her when she said, "Stefan told me you played fantastic yesterday."

"I'm glad to hear it. He's a fine player himself."

She said gently, "I'm sorry I wasn't there."

I thought: Aha.

We walked along in silence a little farther, then she asked, "Do you think you'll miss me? If you leave?"

I said, "Of course I'll miss you."

I didn't sound at all like I meant it.

She said, "You don't have to leave right away, you know."

"Warsaw's a little too cold."

"I meant back in Holland," she said.

I didn't say anything.

"Where are you going to go?"

"I haven't decided yet. Perhaps I'll stay in Amsterdam."

"That would make Benjamin happy." She paused. "I could come along on tour with you sometimes."

"You'd get in the way. What would you do?"

She said mischievously, "I could polish your clarinet."

She made me the same offer two hours later when we finally reached the flat in a taxi. She wanted to play that old game one last time, the game she'd barely won back in New York—where she did her naked best to arouse me, straddling, hovering, teasing, whatever it took without touching me.

This time I won.

I flew out of Warsaw (avoiding Ulrik) during a blizzard the day after the New Year. Maja stayed on, and by the time she returned to Amsterdam I'd moved to Brussels.

For years, trying to explain Maja in memory, I persuaded myself that I used her as an excuse to leave New York. In this version of events I knew what I was doing; I convinced myself via my love for her, or my obsession, to propel myself to Europe because that's what I'd secretly wanted all along, from long before we even met. I deliberately used her as a way out, a means of escape—just as, seemingly, Maja used me as a convenient excuse to leave Simon.

To believe otherwise, after all, would be to admit there'd been feeling in us for each other that I wasn't ready to understand, that I still couldn't hear clearly or know what to do with.

After a year I was getting decent jazz work all around the

continent. My second summer I even played the Montreux festival. I had a regular classical chair with a first-rate radio orchestra in Belgium—meaning we primarily made recordings and broadcasts, but rarely performed. Brussels didn't have much personality, but I was seldom there for any length of time, and it served as a hub for London, Paris, Berlin, and the rest. Even Amsterdam every now and then: I saw Benjamin twice (an afternoon movie, a museum) but not his mother—Maja had snagged a Dutch boyfriend. I stayed in Brussels nearly three years in all, then moved to Paris.

Nothing significant came of my Warsaw recording in the outer world. I shopped the tape around to the important jazz labels in the States for a while until a small independent German label put it out, on record and cassette only, and it vanished immediately, a souvenir of a bygone electronics age. I bought up the last two hundred copies, and saw that a dozen made it back into the hands of the only Poles I felt I understood.

But I was a different player afterwards; I'd felt I had to make a recording under my own name to prove I even existed. In those extreme circumstances, groping around for music on a frozen Warsaw day among absolute strangers, I sounded more like myself than I ever had before, or ever would have surrounded by familiar colleagues in a familiar studio in New York—Maja had called that one right. I played exceptionally well on that cold day because there was no escaping the situation I was in by glibly pretending I knew where I was, no way to play myself around the difficulties. That one session reminded me how good I could really be.

Eventually I learned how little difference a single recording makes to most careers, but at least I'd finally settled into playing only like myself. And the point of making a record-

ing, it seems to me (after several more), is only this: to preserve all you understood on one particular day, to improvise
out of thin air what you felt at that moment in your life,
to reveal it totally, with no apologies and no pretense of
understanding more than you did, and no attempt to look
away from what you didn't want to admit. To be able to
put it all eloquently in the open, hiding nothing, so you can
start afresh.

And with the passage of ten years, that Warsaw recording
swelled until it was most of what I remembered of Poland.
My acute recollections of a single day's improvised music
conveniently obscured all the rest of why I'd actually been
there. I went a long time without bothering to listen to the
original tape of the session (why dig it out?)—not wanting
to hear what else it might tell me.

Then only recently I caught myself remembering Maja
more and more, when it turned out I would be going back
to Poland in June to play at a Cracow arts festival.

All was transformed there, amid all I remembered: a glo-
rious spring, young people about, an awakened old city that
seemed to have risen from the dead, the medieval square
now full of art galleries and well-stocked bookshops and
people saying whatever they wanted in the cafés. Much was
the same: the men still wearing those funny white socks, the
wheedling cream and blue trams, the old intensity still un-
relieved in every glance, every overheard conversation. The
flocks of Polish children led reverently around the gray castle of warrior-kings and the mystical churches which I re-
called as swathed in mists. The waitresses as lovely and
unattainable as ever at my dear Café Marzipan.

The conservatory told me they didn't have my grandfather's name anywhere in its records—much less any of his
compositions preserved. For that matter, they didn't have

his friend Dilko's name listed either, and it made me wonder how much was family legend, and nothing more.

I performed in a fifteenth-century hall with a jazz trio, and was disappointed to see that none of the Polish musicians I knew were playing in the festival. Their old telephone numbers in Warsaw rang and rang or else were answered with an indignation that returned me to that December day of blizzards and urined hallways, trudging around looking for the unfindable. Makowicz had returned to play in Cracow the week before; I wondered how the country looked to him.

And behind my thinking, always, was Maja.

When I performed I imagined I glimpsed her and then lost her in the audience. In sunlight I kept expecting to turn a corner and see her laughing, tantalizingly dressed for warm weather. She'd not have aged a day, of course. We'd take a lemonade somewhere, in a courtyard café with a fountain trilling and a blind accordionist singing, and that evening we'd make love and find out how completely or how little the years had changed us.

I realized, back in Paris, that I didn't have her address anymore. I made some calls and learned that the Dutch government had moved her at last, to a flat of her own; I didn't try her number. Even though photography had worked out unexpectedly well for her, she was still "trapped in herself," as an old friend put it. So when I tried to imagine her as she must be now, for the first time in many years I found myself threading the original reel-to-reel tape of that recording session—and before I knew it Maja came flowing back to me like a flesh-and-blood apparition. Long-legged, grinning, arguing, with all her abracadabra intact. Our days and nights together emerged in a jumble as I listened, and made no sense, made only a nostalgic regret for that time.

How exotic we'd seemed to each other at first. It shook
me now to realize how little difference there'd actually been
then between us. So much of what I was drawn to in her—
the need to keep moving, to avoid coming to grips or being
pinned down; the easy, paralyzed assurance of the nomad—
had been me, a way of justifying myself to myself, a dangerous self-love. I saw now that she'd been attracted to me
for the same reasons, and as soon as she had me, she grew
tired of me, because she was already so deeply tired of herself. It hadn't been Poland I was chasing in her, but a
darker homeland—and had she been less totalitarian, or
had I been better at playing her games, I might not have
broken free.

And as I listened more to the original tape, beneath the
longing I heard suffusing my own playing on that winter
day, I began to hear also a particular, almost reluctant
beauty I'd forgotten was in the music.

Her beauty. Perhaps no one else would've heard it; I had
thought it banished from my memory, but there she was as
I'd wished her to remain, preserved right alongside the
painful person I had come to know. Was it still self-love, to
hear again how much I had once loved someone I had long
thought vanished?

It almost made me want to see her again. She will be
forty-three now; I am sure she is still in superb shape, but
what else will show on her face? Benjamin must be nineteen
and lanky, as tall as his mother, doubtless having added a
language or two to those he already spoke. Does he resonate
to her as the great gift and achievement of those years? I
don't imagine Maja with any one man beside her, but still
lover after lover.

And a day may come, perhaps already has come, when
there is no one new, no one different, no one better—and
the strength she felt most deeply was hers may not have

survived. I wonder: does she see herself reflected in Amsterdam shop windows, flashing past on a bicycle, and look away?

Does she ever think on me?

Or perhaps, having listened too much to one day's music, hearing only what I wished to hear, I have got it all wrong.